D0560317

ROCK RIVER

RanVan

A Worthy Opponent

BOOKS BY
Diana Wieler

RanVan: The Defender
RanVan: A Worthy Opponent
RanVan: Magic Nation

Last Chance Summer
Bad Boy

Ran Van

A Worthy Opponent

◆

DIANA WIELER

A GROUNDWOOD BOOK
Douglas & McIntyre
TORONTO / VANCOUVER / BUFFALO

Groundwood Books / Douglas & McIntyre Ltd.
585 Bloor Street West, Toronto, Ontario M6G 1K5

Distributed in the U.S.A. by Publishers Group West
4065 Hollis Street, Emeryville, CA 94608

We acknowledge the support of the Canada Council for the Arts
and the Ontario Arts Council for our publishing program.

Library of Congress Data is available

Canadian Cataloguing in Publication Data

Wieler, Diana J. (Diana Jean), 1961-
RanVan a worthy opponent
"A Groundwood book".
ISBN 0-88899-271-8
I. Title.
PS8595.I53143R36 1997   jC813'.54   C97-931606-5
PZ7.W54Ra 1997

Cover illustration by Ludmilla Temertey
Cover photograph by Emilio De Cesaris,
Tony Stone Images
Design by Michael Solomon
Printed and bound in Canada

For Ben,
my expert on video games,
superheroes and good and evil.

ONE

O, valiant warrior, we've long awaited your arrival! Our benevolent ruler has been overpowered by his evil twin and now serves the forces of darkness. Together the brothers are invincible. Their magic holds sway over both the planet and its inhabitants. Our world is in chaos.

Rhan Van gripped the edges of the game console. He'd wandered into the arcade almost idly, a walk to stretch his legs after three cramped days on a Greyhound bus. But dozens of screens glowed brightly in the dim room, and the air was alive with the searing of lasers. At the back of Captain John's he'd come across this game, Gemini Planet, and he'd forgotten about walking anywhere.

He'd liked the graphics instantly. The preview scroll showed the landing of a small dragon-winged craft on a planet sharply halved in black and white. In the next frame the pilot stepped out onto a shadowed landscape. His flight suit was inset with metal plates, but it looked like a knight's armour to Rhan.

The brothers do not rule the sun! Their powers are greatest during the hours of Descent; your own rises during Ascent. The shifting polarity of the planet can be your greatest ally, or your peril.

In the corner of the screen Rhan could see the

7

numbers clicking off at unnatural speed—an hour's worth in the time it took to draw a breath. When 23:59 kicked over, the dark background began to lighten, lush plants grew over the barren rock. The pilot was changing, too. Dull metal gleamed silver and the spaces between the plates began to glow—a liquid, electrified blue. Rhan's heart leapt. It was his colour.

Earn the five rings of Ashtar, hidden above and below ground. They will give you the strength to destroy the evil twin and release our king. But pursue your foe with care: the brothers are identical. Your choice will lead either to glory or to night neverending.

Great, Rhan thought. The guy you have to rescue looks exactly like the guy you're trying to kill off. And the privilege of saving the planet wasn't cheap, either. Four quarters to start, two to continue. His mind reeled thinking what it would cost to learn the moves, never mind get good at them.

But he wasn't just anybody. Under the code name RanVan he'd blazed a lot of different video battlefields in his career. He was coordinated and he learned fast—better than fast.

"Don't mind me. I love to watch amateurs get fried by this thing."

Rhan spun around. A young man was leaning against a pillar, arms folded over his chest. He seemed slightly older than Rhan—seventeen, maybe—and he was taller but lean. At first glance Rhan thought the stranger was bald, but then he

8

noticed the white, almost translucent fuzz over his skull. He could have been an android, except for the eyes: bright and steady, intensely alive.

"What makes you think I'm an amateur?" Rhan said.

The stranger suddenly flipped a dollar coin at him. "Go for it," he said.

The challenge was sharp in the air. Part of Rhan wanted to dive into Gemini Planet then and there and blast the micro chips right out of the thing. But reality set in. He didn't know the first moves on this game, and he wasn't about to die horribly for this jerk's entertainment.

Rhan tossed the money back, just as fast. "Sorry, I'm not taking students this year."

The young man almost smiled as he tucked the coin in his pocket. He gestured at the scores monitor that had just come up on Gemini Planet's screen. It listed the top twenty players, under their code names.

"That's funny," he said, "because I know everybody up there and you're not one of them."

"I'm incognito. Keeps back the crowd." Rhan was curious now but he tried to be casual. "So where are you?"

No change of expression. Rhan scanned the list of code names.

"DayGlo?" he said, picking one from the middle. There was no response. "Hakker? Merlin?"

"Today I brew, tomorrow I bake..." the stranger said.

Rhan stared. For an instant he thought he recognized the curious phrase. But then it was lost.

"Figure it out, *amateur*," the stranger said. "Use your brain, if you can." He slipped easily through the players and into the mall.

Just then, the lights flickered rapidly.

"Time, guys!" the attendant called.

Rhan blinked. Damn! The place was closing and he hadn't played anything. As he left the arcade he gave Gemini Planet a backward glance, the word "amateur" curdling in his stomach. He was pretty sure which monitor RanVan was going to conquer first.

Outside Captain John's, Rhan paused to light a cigarette. Around him the mall was a din of rattling screens and doors as shops closed up for the night.

Across from the arcade, a small cluster of guys in sports jackets had formed a ring out from a bare wall. Rhan remembered passing them earlier, at the mall entrance, and he'd given himself a mental warning. Sixteen years in Vancouver had taught him to thread his way around the various packs that staked out the malls and school courtyards. If the circle closed on you, you'd lose something: jacket, shoes, money. Or you'd just lose.

They had quarry now. Shoppers heading for the doors gave the group a wide berth. The attendant from Captain John's wandered into the doorway to watch.

Then, the first shove. The ring of jackets broke

for an instant and Rhan caught a glimpse inside. The little guy in the Toledo Mud Hens baseball jacket barely came up to their chins. He was just a kid! In a panicked push he tried to force his way out of the circle and was yanked back, hard. The cluster tightened again.

Rhan looked left and right, his pulse in his temples. The mall was full of people. Why didn't somebody do something?

He thrust his cigarette in the ashtray without looking at it. He could feel the familiar roar beginning in his veins, the first gust of energy shaking him awake. He was needed here. When he started to move, the rush intensified, each step accelerating the next, like running down a hill.

There's five of them—five on two. Think fast! What have you got, RanVan? Something, anything!

The element of surprise. Rhan hit the leader at a dead run, a shoulder check into the broad back that sent them both sprawling onto the polished floor. But the impact had wrenched the circle apart. The others stumbled, dazed.

"Go!" Rhan called.

The kid bolted for open space. Rhan scrambled to get up, but he felt hands seize the back of his jacket. A blaze of fury drove up from his stomach. They might take him, but RanVan the Defender wasn't going down without a fight.

The instant he was hauled to his feet, Rhan whipped around with his elbow up—and drove it into the security guard's stomach.

11

Rhan Van had turned sixteen on Halloween, on a Greyhound bus travelling from Vancouver to Thunder Bay. He had dark hair to his shoulders, and metal frame glasses. He wasn't big but he prided himself on being quick, nimble.

Riding home in the police car, Rhan knew he'd have to be more than nimble to wriggle out of this.

The cruiser hesitated in the parking lot of the Trail's End Motel, which had been Rhan's new address for less than five hours. The officer looked over the line of ten faded clapboard cabins.

"Which suite did you say your grandmother was in?" he asked.

"We're not in a suite, we live in the house," Rhan said irritably from the back seat. "My gran's cousin owns the place."

They pulled up to the main doors, a reception area that had been built on the front of the old two-storey house.

"You know, this really isn't *necessary*," Rhan said. "You don't want to shock her or anything. She's got a bad heart." Not really a lie. Didn't everybody over sixty have a bad heart?

"Uh-huh," the officer said, unimpressed. "Let's go, son."

Gran came to the door in a housecoat, an imposing five foot eight even in slippers. Her wild white hair was rolled up in curlers and tied

with a blue kerchief. She listened intently but didn't say much. That, Rhan knew, would come later.

"There aren't going to be charges laid," the officer was telling Gran, "but there could have been, if you get my drift. I think the security guard is being very nice about this. Maybe it was a misunderstanding, but assault is assault."

"It wasn't assault, it was a rescue," Rhan said.

"And I thought you ought to know what kind of crowd is up there at the mall. We've had one bad incident after another: fights, theft. It's not a group I'd let my kid hang around with."

"I'm not hanging around with anybody. I just got here! I told you, it was a rescue!"

They both glared at him. Rhan folded his arms over his chest and shut up.

When the policeman left, Gran said nothing. All the way up to his room on the second floor, she didn't speak. Rhan tried to rehearse his argument in his head but found he couldn't concentrate. He knew he was in for it. Why didn't she just start, already?

When the door closed, he turned to her. She was wiping at her eyes with a tissue.

"What the hell..?" Rhan started, alarmed.

"Well, what do you think?" Gran said. "I open the door and all I see's a uniform."

"I was right there behind him," Rhan said.

"I couldn't see you. And no cop ever brought me good news."

It was true. With a pang Rhan realized what she must have thought in those few seconds—that he was hurt, or worse. The scare wasn't completely gone from her face.

"I'm sorry," he said.

Gran tucked the tissue into her pocket. "Seems like you got a lot to be sorry for tonight."

Rhan sighed. "Look, what was I supposed to do? Stand there and watch this kid get beat up—?"

"No," Gran cut him off. "But you don't have to jump in with both feet. What do you think security guards are for? Why didn't you just go get one?"

Rhan didn't answer. In the mall that thought hadn't even crossed his mind. He sat down on the bed. It was hard and spare, like the rest of the little room. There was an old brown dresser and a wooden chair.

Gran was looking out the window. "Like it isn't hard enough to be here in the first place?" she said. "You don't know what it did to me to ask that woman for a place to stay."

"You're the one who keeps saying it's only temporary," Rhan said.

"And it is," Gran replied with conviction. "Believe me, Zoe was the last resort. If the Devil himself had come up with a better idea I would've considered it. It just all happened too fast."

Only two weeks earlier Gran had been the caretaker of the ramshackle six-plex where they'd lived in Vancouver. When it was sold, she'd lost

her job and her home in one swoop.

"That Zoe has to see you trucked home by the police," Gran continued, "like some common hooligan..."

"Right. I'm an *un*common hooligan."

"Don't get smart. You know what I mean. It scares me, this temper of yours."

Rhan got to his feet. "It's not temper..."

"You're belting people for fun?"

"It was an accident, for Christ's sake!"

"You gotta be standing on the track to get hit by the train," Gran shot back.

Her blue eyes were clear now. Rhan turned away.

"Sometimes you make me proud and sometimes you just make me wonder," Gran said after a moment. Her voice softened. "Kid, I need you to grow up."

The fiery knot in his throat was sudden, unexpected. When he heard the door close, he dropped onto the bed again.

Rhan Van had known he was a knight for a little over a month. There had been a girl in Vancouver and he'd thought she was in trouble. Wanting to help her, trying to save her, he'd discovered something in him that was extraordinary.

He wasn't exactly sure how he did it, but when the power overtook him, amazing things happened. In the past few rollercoaster weeks he'd pushed over a wall with his bare hands and saved a man from plunging off the third storey of a

house. The night he and Gran left for Thunder Bay, he'd stopped a robbery with a well-aimed can of soup.

The transformation was always brief, but in his mind's eye he could see the electric blue energy running over him like armour; he could feel it zinging through his veins. In those moments he was RanVan the Defender. He was somebody who could help, who could make the difference. It was the greatest feeling in the world.

Even tonight, before everything got so screwed up.

He winced. He remembered the jarring impact, and the way the old security guard had crumpled and fallen to his knees. Over and over Rhan had said he was sorry, babbling on, shocked. He hadn't known he could hit anyone that hard.

Somehow he had to get a grip on this. He was still a knight, he just wasn't ...finished. He needed training—a teacher or something. But he didn't know where to look, and it couldn't wait.

He stood suddenly and rummaged in the dresser drawer for a notepad and pencil. He hesitated, then started to write.

1. Perfect existing skills. That was the biggie, Rhan thought grimly. He had to figure out how to control the power. He couldn't let it get away on him, like tonight. There had to be a way to help people without hurting anybody.

2. Determine parameters. Being a knight was so

new, maybe there were parts he hadn't discovered yet. What could he do and what was impossible? He had to know where the edges were.

3. Pain. A whole category in a single word. Rhan knew he had too many mortal genes to be impervious to pain, but he figured a real knight would be pretty nonchalant about it. It was a mark of the breed.

4. Select quest. That was a future thing, distant and blurry, to look at once he'd conquered everything else. Knights always had quests—golden fleeces, holy grails. It was the journey that started the great adventure of your life.

Rhan read his plan over and over, feeling a strange tingle. Words became different when you wrote them down. It wasn't just a list any more, it was a vow. And a vow was something you kept...or else.

But he had no idea what "else" might be.

TWO

OHM mani padme humm ohm mani padme humm ohm mani padme humm...

The sound stole into Rhan's sleep, nagging him awake. What a lousy dream, he thought, rolling over. But the noise kept on—not words so much as a moan, twisted into syllables. He propped himself up on his elbow. It wasn't his imagination and it wasn't going away.

Ohm mani padme humm ohm mani padme humm ohm mani padme humm...

Christ, that was irritating!

Rhan pulled on a pair of sweatpants and his glasses, glancing out the window of his room. The sun was barely a fiery edge on the distant hills. He dragged himself out into the hallway and almost bumped into Gran, still in her nightgown.

"What is that godawful noise?" she said.

"Sounds like a broken record."

"Or a cat in heat." Gran looked around suspiciously. "I wouldn't put it past her to have a *cat*."

Rhan led the way downstairs and they moved cautiously through the dim house. The sound seemed to be coming from a small room that Zoe had said was used for storage—brooms, cleaners, extra towels for the suites. The door was closed.

Rhan hesitated but Gran stepped past him,

18

turned the knob and gingerly pushed the door open a few inches.

The little room was lit only by three candles. Peering over Gran's shoulder, Rhan could just make out Zoe in a nightshirt, her face lifted toward the ceiling as she said the words over and over.

Ohm mani padme humm...

Gran yanked the door shut. She gripped Rhan's arm, her face pale.

"We're gettin' outta here right now. The woman is a devil-worshipper!"

Before he could answer, the storage room opened again. Zoe stood with one hand on her hip.

"*That* is a Tibetan serenity chant, I'll have you know, not devil worship. I always chant at dawn."

"That noise—serenity?" Gran said. "Just for who, I'd like to know."

"For the lady who owns the house," Zoe snapped. "Who asks that you show a little common decency and not invade her privacy," she added, looking directly at Rhan.

She flounced past them, heading for the stairway. Gran turned suddenly on Rhan.

"You got that? Don't open any doors!"

He threw up his hands. "You did it—not me!"

Gran didn't seem to hear. "Don't you worry, kid. I'll get us out of here, just as soon as I can. I won't have you exposed to...God knows what."

As Zoe strode up the stairs Rhan watched her

intently. Gran had said her cousin was about ten years behind her, and Rhan had been expecting a senior citizen. Now he didn't know if the term applied.

A half hour later, Zoe had changed her clothes and her mood. In a crisp white shirt and blue jeans, she nodded politely in their direction before she made her toast. She had Gran's broad-shouldered height and the same square jaw, but the resemblance ended there. Her hair was more pepper than salt, a wiry ripple that flared out in a wedge just below her ears. She wore no makeup except for red lipstick, too bright but stylish in a way. She didn't *look* like she chanted in broom closets.

"So what's the plan for today?" Zoe said.

"I don't have what you'd call a plan," Gran said a little stiffly. "But I was outside for a look at them suites. I was thinking maybe they could use a good cleaning. It's our specialty, you know."

Rhan was insulted, but so was Zoe.

"That's just the paint," Zoe said briskly. "They're clean inside. I have a girl who comes..."

"Then you'd better fire her. I could see the dust through the window." Gran was warming up now. This was her kind of topic. "When was the last time you shampooed the rugs?"

Zoe opened her mouth, then shut it.

"That's what I thought," Gran said. She put her hand on Rhan's shoulder. "Good thing we got an expert here."

"Thanks a lot," he grumbled when he and Gran were alone. "Maybe I was looking forward to a career change."

"We gotta pitch in," Gran said. "Do our part. I'm not going to the grave owing that woman a dime."

Zoe offered to rent a carpet steamer from the grocery store, and then invited them along for the drive, as a tour of the city. The November sky was fiercely blue as they headed out to her sporty hatchback, but there was more in the air than autumn. Gran stopped in her tracks.

"Jesus, Mary and Joseph! What's that stink?"

"It's like somebody put a dead goat in a wet paper bag and lit it on fire," Rhan said.

Zoe smiled grimly as she swung into the driver's seat. "*That*, everyone in Thunder Bay will tell you, is the smell of money. To the rest of the world it's just paper mills."

As they drove, Rhan could easily see the edges of civilization, where the landscape rose up in tree-heavy foothills. After Vancouver's sprawling maze of streets and suburbs, Thunder Bay struck him as temporary, a work camp. They passed large homes and bright storefronts, but the skyline was jobs, from the soaring grain terminals at the port to the smokestacks of the largest mill.

"Actually, it really isn't one city, it's two," Zoe said. "Port Arthur and Fort William. Or, depending which side you live on, Poor Arthur and William's Fart."

21

"Zoe was always the *lady* in the family," Gran said under her breath.

"How come it just goes under one name, then?" Rhan asked.

"Togetherness," Zoe said. "The two towns always squabbled over everything so they voted on one name, as part of a big unity drive. They even built a shopping centre right between the towns, to draw people from both sides. With this mall, I thee wed."

The next minute, though, Zoe seemed to regret the bad review she was giving. Thunder Bay, she said, had a lot going for it. Aside from the Lake Superior port and the paper mills, there were amethyst fields and skiing to draw the tourists. Mount McKay, she said proudly, was a world-class site for Nordic ski jumping.

Rhan leaned his head against the window to get a better view of the dark, flat-topped hump beyond the city's edge. He'd spent his life within sight of the Rockies—real mountains with majestic peaks and Technicolor shades. Mount McKay struck him as ominous—hulking and half-finished.

"Looks like a bad haircut," Gran said dryly. "A little too much off the top."

When they got back, Rhan followed his grandmother out to the first cabin, trundling the perky, user-friendly rug steamer along behind him. It was far newer than anything he was used to. But the rugs were worse.

"What do you think?" Gran asked, setting

down an armload of cleaners.

Rhan glanced around at the twenty-year-old lamp and night table, the ghastly flowered bedspread, the tin ashtrays. The room smelled like people passing through, or old clothes that had been in a drawer for a long time.

"We didn't bring the right equipment," he said. "We need something bigger—like a bulldozer."

"Now, don't be too hard. It must have been real quaint in its day."

"I've heard of that day—the Mesozoic."

"Oh, get to work, you." Gran snapped a rag at him, grinning.

Rhan swung into action and the familiar details came back to him: the numbing vibration, the roar, the constant changing of filthy water for fresh. No wonder he hated it.

But once he'd gotten the hang of it again, it didn't require consciousness. He found himself thinking about the game he'd seen in the arcade. Gemini Planet had caught his imagination: the lone pilot, the shifting landscape, even the twin kings—one to deliver and one to destroy.

He wondered about going to the mall. He hadn't made any friends last night; there could be trouble. But even thinking like that made him mad. It was too much like giving up. A knight might lose, but he didn't surrender. Ever.

It was mid-afternoon when Gran sat down wearily on one of the beds. She lit a cigarette, and

23

the sudden scent almost lifted Rhan out of his shoes. His own package was tucked away in his room, out of sight but not out of mind.

"That's bloody well enough for one day, if you ask me," she said. "We can't even get to number eight and number ten until the folks check out."

"The steamer's rented until Tuesday," Rhan said hopefully.

"And you've got school on Monday."

"I'll make the sacrifice."

"No, you won't," Gran said. "You've missed enough as it is, with this move and all. I don't want you getting so far behind you can't catch up."

You only had to worry about catching up, Rhan thought, when you were going in the same direction. But he didn't say it. The school argument was an old one.

He whipped out an imaginary pad.

"Now, about your bill," he said cheerfully. "That's five hours at $5.75, plus GST and PST, plus my tip..."

Gran didn't smile. "Kid, I don't got it. And if I had it, I'd need it. Pretty much everything I had saved up, I spent getting us here."

Rhan watched the blue-white trail of smoke rise into the air. Cleaning rugs for Gran had always been a source of income for him, his only source. And even though he wasn't dead broke yet, he was getting there. It scared him to imagine being without money. He could tell it scared her, too.

Rhan shrugged. "I guess I'll just hang around today."

Gran tossed him a cigarette from her pack. "Just as well," she said with a faint smile. "I think I'll have a whole lot more *serenity* if I've got you in my sight."

THREE

B Y 9:25 Monday morning, Rhan was leaving the main office of McKay Senior High. He had his list of classes, locker assignment, textbooks and a note of admission. He'd expected his registration to take most of the morning, not to be whipped through in under half an hour.

Computers, he thought, had a dark side.

He dropped off the books he didn't need and wandered through the empty hallways, stalling. School had been getting harder every year—not the work, but just showing up. It hadn't always been that way. He remembered how it used to be a kind of contest for him—how fast he could finish his work, how high a grade he could get. He'd soared through elementary and most of junior high like a runner trying to beat his personal best.

And then, somewhere in grade eight, he'd figured it out. There was no prize. His mark on a page—or a report card—didn't seem like a real thing. He could work hard, he could be great, but it had to be *for* something, and a number just wasn't enough. After that the race had become a treadmill, and he'd found himself getting off it, a lot. He couldn't help but wonder how soon he could get off it permanently.

A metallic *ka-ching* turned his head. To his right, a young man burst into the school, hair wild

from the wind, brown leather jacket flapping open. He sprinted a few paces and stopped short. A stretch of floor had recently been mopped, the wet area staked out with warning pylons. Brown Jacket stared intently at the pylons, then noticed Rhan.

"Hey...hey, you!" he called.

Rhan took a cautious step. "What?"

"Do me a favour. Run down to the office. Tell them a guy slipped and hit his head."

"Where? Out on the steps?"

"No, right there." The young man gestured at the gleaming floor. "Any second now."

"You're going to fake a fall," Rhan said, catching on. "What for?"

"What do you care what for?"

"Because I only *lie* when it's a worthy cause."

"Well, how about my whole future, is that worthy enough for you? How about I've already had three lates and this one's gonna be a suspension? Unless I come up with a good excuse, like a concussion," he added, looking at the floor again.

"Good excuse," Rhan repeated. "Yeah, it's so good they'll call your parents to tell them about it—right after the ambulance gets here."

"Well, shit. What am I going to do? My balls are bookends now."

Pressure. What was the guy looking at him for? And yet at the same time Rhan could feel the wheels turning inside him, revving to the sudden challenge.

"Okay, what about this. I'm new here." He rat-

tled the note of admission. "And somebody at the office told you to get me to my first class. Except I slipped on the wet floor and twisted my ankle. And you couldn't leave me stranded and that's why we're so late. Get the instructor to phone down to your class."

Brown Jacket ran his hand nervously through his hair. "I don't know. Cherneski's pretty sharp."

"Fine, forget it." Rhan shrugged as he backed away. "I have to get to class."

"Okay, okay! We'll try it. Give me your books. And grab a hold of my shoulder. This better look good."

Rhan limped all the way to his first class, Chem 101 with Mr. Laos, just to get into character. The teacher looked concerned but he threw them a curve.

"Geez, J.R.! Why didn't you take him to the nurse's office?"

"He says it's not that bad," J.R. said quickly. "Just aggravated an old football injury."

Oh, *right*, Rhan thought. He was five foot five and weighed 130 pounds soaking wet. He hated to think of a team desperate enough to have him. He thrust out his note of admission before Laos could think of that, too.

The paper did the trick. "New students," the teacher grumbled. "Why didn't I get a call about this? Nobody tells me anything. How do they even know I have a spare desk?!"

Laos motioned Rhan in to find a seat and then

phoned down to J.R.'s class, explaining the delay and griping a little. By the time he turned back to teaching, the buzzer had sounded and the class leapt up eagerly, before he could assign any work.

Rhan limped out behind the crowd, buoyed by success and the happy noise ahead of him. It was, he decided, a textbook-style rescue. Clean, controlled. Everybody wins, nobody gets hurt.

At the end of the day, Rhan was leaving through the main doors when a voice called him over to the parking lot. J.R. was leaning against the driver's door of a shiny black four-by-four truck, his thumbs hooked easily on the pockets of his leather aviator's jacket. His lank hair was combed back, effortlessly in place, a pale brown that looked as if it could lighten by a single day in the sun.

"Hey, hey! It's the man himself. How's the bum leg, bud?"

Rhan threw his hands into the air. "I can walk! It's a miracle!"

J.R. laughed. "It worked, you know. Cherneski never even blinked when I got to her class." He grabbed the truck's door handle, then stopped. "Hey, you need a lift somewhere? I'm going now. I could drop you off."

For a moment Rhan didn't answer. He wasn't used to being offered things, certainly not rides. In Vancouver, he hadn't been on speaking terms with anyone who owned a vehicle—and it hadn't mattered to him a bit. But suddenly the black truck

with monster tires and chrome roll bar was calling to him. More than fast, it looked dangerous.

He shrugged. "Yeah, sure."

J.R. Payne, Rhan learned, was in grade eleven, but he also worked part-time at the biggest mill in Thunder Bay.

"Over the summer I was ninth helper on a line at the sawmill, but now I'm general labour, some nights and weekends." J.R. grinned. "Just a grunt. Except I almost lost it today," he continued. "If I'd been suspended, my parents would've made me quit. And that'd be the end of this baby." He patted the dashboard. "You saved my ass this morning and that's a fact."

The four-by-four didn't need speed to turn heads. One look and pedestrians scrambled out of the way. Only at traffic lights did J.R. gun the engine, a quick burst to make sure he was first off the mark. Rhan didn't have his licence yet but he began to think about it. Driving, he decided, could be fun.

"So, like, who are you, anyway?" J.R. said.

Rhan told him.

"Whoa, strange. That's Arab, right?"

Rhan sighed inwardly. He always got stuff like this.

"No, we're from a small country that borders the Pacific Ocean," he said.

"Oh, yeah?"

"It was a primitive paradise until the tourists came and destroyed our traditional way of life."

"Yeah?"

"It's called Vancouver," Rhan said.

For three full seconds J.R. was silent—and then he got it. "You almost had me going there," he said. He smiled and shook his head. "You're twisted, bud."

And J.R. was a natural straight man, Rhan thought. But that wasn't a bad thing.

When the four-by-four pulled into the Trail's End, Rhan felt a pang. From the cab of the truck the weatherstained clapboard looked shabbier than when he'd left this morning. But J.R. surveyed the line of suites and smiled wickedly.

"Looks like ten good dates, all in a row," he said.

When Rhan climbed out of the truck, J.R. unrolled his window.

"We'll see you around, hey?"

He said it like he meant it, like he was looking forward to it. Rhan was surprised. He wasn't used to this, either. "Yeah, sure."

J.R. hesitated. "Tell me something. Are those cabins always full? I mean, you sometimes have vacancies, right?"

"Sometimes," Rhan said. Actually, Zoe was thrilled to have four suites rented at a time.

J.R. lowered his voice. "Well, if you could get an extra key to your old friend J.R., him and this certain special girl would be real obliged."

Rhan stepped back, stung. J.R. misunderstood.

"Well, try anyway, okay? Good man!"

31

J.R. glanced at the row of suites once more, then whipped into a smart U-turn and sailed out into the street.

Gran was in the kitchen, ironing pillow cases. She'd been pressing when Rhan had left this morning and she was still at it. Never mind all the suites they'd cleaned and the two rugs he still had to do tonight. He felt suddenly, painfully used.

"First day okay?" Gran said. He could hear the hope in her voice.

"Yeah, great," he snapped. "I took over the main office and burnt it to the ground—before lunch."

Gran looked up from the pillow case, but he was already gone.

FOUR

RanVan was fighting, flailing, clawing wildly for the surface as bubbles of air bled out from under his helmet and rose slowly through the murky liquid. The harder he struggled, the deeper he seemed to sink. Gemini Planet had become Gemini Bog.

Quicksand. You should have known, tinhead.

The smooth ground had looked too inviting after the boulder-strewn terrain he'd just left. But he'd been frantic to get out of there. He'd almost exhausted his laser power fighting off the flying bat creatures that dove at him as he struggled around the boulders, and night was coming on. He'd already found out that everything got bigger—and meaner—during Descent.

He'd gotten out by 11:56. At 12:05 the ground had begun to soften; by 12:30 he was sinking. Now the porridge landscape surrounded him, the gunmetal and tar colours of his suit reminding him that he was at his lowest physical strength.

Great. Weak and stuck. You should have taken your chances with the B-52 bats.

In the back of his mind he seemed to remember to keep still, that movement only sucked you down faster in quicksand. But he was driven on by a sense of dread. The screen clock was still running at its supernatural speed toward 00:01.

33

What would happen if he was still in this gook when Ascent began?

He reached the bottom just as the new day kicked over. The quicksand hardened to rock around him the same instant he saw the door. He watched the empowerment colours light up his immobolized knight, frozen in a pitiful stretch toward escape.

Stupid! All the time he'd wasted thrashing around, when he could have reached the portal and been through. In his guts he knew it led to something important, or they wouldn't have gone to the trouble to hide it.

But time was hurtling on. *Continue?* the screen blinked. *Deposit two coins...10...9...8...*

Rhan checked his pockets frantically, but he was done. He'd brought ten dollars with him tonight and the machine had it all now. He gripped the console of Gemini Planet while the seconds counted down. Like being in a vivid dream, it was hard to wake up and let go.

When his score came on, he saw that he was just over 400,000 points. Not a bad start, but the bottom of the standings was a million plus. Oh, well, he was the only one who knew.

"Hey, it's you."

Rhan swung around. The kid was standing behind him, still wearing the Toledo Mud Hens jacket. This close, he looked even smaller: the cuffs of the big jacket lapped over his knuckles. Grade school, Rhan thought. Eleven, maybe twelve. He was suddenly glad about the rescue, no matter how it had turned out. The poor little guy would have been doomed.

"So, you got a death wish or were you just stoned?"

"What?" Rhan said.

"I mean, my ass was grass, okay? But you kinda lucked out. We only had five. I've seen Jimbo run twelve at a time. But it was kinda stupid, okay?"

"Thanks," Rhan said grimly. "I live to serve."

"What?"

"Never mind. What was he after you for, anyway?"

"Jimbo? He wants the jacket."

Rhan nodded. He'd suspected as much. "Thought it was his size?"

"Uh...it is...kinda."

The kid smirked, and Rhan suddenly knew.

"You stole it? He was trying to get back his own jacket?!"

"Hey, he ripped it off from somebody else," the kid said, stepping back. "And you never asked, you know?"

The stab of truth deflated Rhan. The kid was right. He'd charged into last week's rescue full throttle, no questions asked. Talk about tinheads. He'd elbowed an innocent old man in the stomach to save a thief. He started to button his jacket. Go home, Van. Tie yourself to the bed.

"Hey, you got a car?" the kid said.

"No."

"Dope?"

"No!"

"Smokes?"

"Not for you," Rhan shot back. "Christ, what a mooch!"

The kid grinned. "That's me—the sponge. Hey, how're you doing on this thing?" he asked, stepping past Rhan and gripping the controls to Gemini Planet.

Rhan felt a spark of hope. "Not bad. You play this one?"

"Beat it," Sponge said.

"Bull!"

Sponge stuck out his hand for money. Rhan was already reaching into his pocket before he realized what the kid was doing—and remembered he was broke anyway.

"You little...sponge!" Rhan said, but it was hard not to laugh. The kid was persistent.

Sponge leaned against the console. "Listen, I mean it. I'll use your code. You can even do the last battle if you want. But you pay my way and I'll get you there."

"*I'll* get me there," Rhan said, and the determined sound in his voice surprised him.

It surprised the kid, too. He looked at Rhan with new interest. "Where are you from?" Sponge said.

Rhan pulled up his jacket collar but didn't answer. Was it that obvious he was an outsider?

36

Sponge was studying him. "Who are you? You're somebody, right?"

"Everybody's somebody," Rhan said, heading for the door. The kid followed him to the arcade exit.

"Jimbo's gonna be looking for you. Watch your back," he said.

Rhan pointed to the crest of the swinging hen. "Better watch your own. He knows it better."

When he stepped out through the mall doors, the cold night air was like a slap on both cheeks. It was going to be a long walk home. Rhan started wearily through the near-empty parking lot.

The past week had felt like a month. The kids at McKay were just as dull and cliquey as the kids in Vancouver. Wrapped up in their jobs and cars and sports, they paid him only the barest notice. "You don't ski? Like, *really?*"

J.R. Payne went out of his way to be friendly, but Rhan avoided him. He wasn't his type of company.

Rhan had needed to get lost tonight, to step out of his life for awhile, and Gemini Planet had worked. He could still feel the pull of the writhing forest he'd hacked his way through in the opening stretch, still remember the rush of excitement when he'd figured out the boulder maze and located the first ring of Ashtar.

In that instant he'd forgotten about Captain John's and the UniCity Mall and even Thunder Bay. Gemini Planet was his planet, and its changing laws of nature were tough but fair. If you learned and adapted, you went on. If you didn't, you were annihilated.

And the constant threat of it, the battle of it—to learn or die—made a connection in him that he couldn't explain. The wires touch, was all he could think.

A set of headlights clicked on, to his right. The beam felt wrong—an odd angle for a parked car—and Rhan quickened his pace to get out of its way. But the light didn't leave him and he could hear the engine now, a deep rumble closing in. Rhan glanced over his shoulder and was blinded by the glare.

He scrambled to the left, but the lights swung over with him, erasing any doubt. This was deliberate, this had to be Jimbo and company. He tore forward in a burst of panic. They wouldn't run him down, would they? There were other people in the parking lot, weren't there? Why didn't somebody help him?!

He only knew one thing for sure: he was dead meat in the open. Somehow he had to get back to the mall. But what if they were waiting for him there, too?

The icy air scraped his throat as he raced in a wide circle toward the mall doors. The driver sensed where he was going and accelerated, pulling up on his left, squeezing off his escape route.

Straight ahead a long wall jutted out abruptly into a right angle—a corner where brick met brick. Rhan threw his arms out to cushion the impact, a body blow that made him stagger back. Dazed, he spun around to face his attackers.

The headlights slowed to a stop, too close to his trembling legs. The heat of the engine rushed up against him in an acrid gust. Rhan was hurting but he was ready—to fight, to run, whatever he had to do to get out of this.

But it was no gang. To his astonishment, he could make out only one figure in the white car. What the hell was going on?

The driver's window unrolled and somebody leaned out.

"I saw your show in the mall last week, amateur. Too bad about that security guard. But I give you an E for effort. It was nice, almost *brave*."

The recognition came over Rhan like a chill. The voice, and the shape of the skull. Under the parking-lot lights the fuzz of hair looked white, translucent.

"It's not enough, though. Can he *think*? That's the question."

"What do you want?" Rhan demanded.

"Now, you didn't get it last time but you've had a week to mull it over," the stranger continued. "And I have a theory, amateur, that people think better under pressure."

He hit the gas and the brake at the same time, a surge and squeal of tires. Rhan threw himself back against the wall, a reflex of self-preservation, but the car crawled only inches.

"Okay, let's try it again," the young man called as he eased back to an idle. *"Today I brew, tomorrow I bake..."*

Nutcase! Rhan thought wildly. This guy was crazy. They'd only had a conversation in an arcade, for Christ's sake. He hadn't done any—

Thunderbolt.

"Tomorrow the queen's child I take," Rhan blurted. He looked into the bright, intent eyes. "Rumpelstiltskin."

The stranger hesitated before he smiled. "See, my theory works. You *can* think if you're scared enough. You have my permission to pursue the game. Surrender now and you're free to go."

The thrill in his voice was unmistakable. Rhan felt the fury wash over him, a burning wave from his stomach to his face. He'd been chased and humiliated and scared to death so this bastard could get his kicks.

"Well, my permission looks like this!" Rhan braced himself against the wall and booted the left headlight with all his might. There was a dull cracking sound under his heel, and then that side went dark. Got him!

But there wasn't a moment to lose. Rhan scrambled over the car hood and vaulted onto the pavement. Then he was blazing a straight line to the nearest edge of the parking lot, a grassy rise across the street from a condo complex. You'll lose him in there, Rhan thought, or at least he can't follow with the car.

He expected his pursuer to be on his heels, but there was no sound except his own runners and his drumming heart. At the top of the knoll he allowed himself a backward glance and stumbled to a stop.

He wasn't being chased. The stranger was outside his car now, calmly inspecting the damage. Rhan stared. He couldn't bring himself to believe the guy had given up.

And while he was standing there, his eyes caught on the white Camaro's personalized licence plate for the first time. He remembered the name from the Gemini Planet scores tracker, ninth from the top.

"That's really too bad," the young man shouted across the parking lot. "You're not thinking again. You know you're going to pay, don't you?"

"Sure. You take VISA?" Rhan called back. He was too far to be threatened, too high from the rush of his escape.

"I'm old-fashioned, amateur. I only take blood. But I'll need some I.D. with that."

"I'll give you a hint, *Iceman*," Rhan shouted back. "Just watch for the guy who bumps your sorry ass right off the screen. Use your brain and figure it out—if you can."

Rhan turned and fled into the maze of condos, his feet barely touching the ground. He was almost home before he realized that smashing something had been the highlight of his whole week. And then he slowed down.

◆

In his room, Rhan sat on the end of the bed, smoking a cigarette in the dark. He had the window open a hand's breadth and the steady draft had chilled the whole room. But he didn't have a choice. There was no ashtray. He wasn't supposed to be smoking up here.

He'd come to Thunder Bay with a small supply of cigarettes and it had been getting smaller ever since. He hadn't found a store yet that would sell to minors and anyway, he was almost out of money. "Borrowing" smokes from Gran had always been his back-up system, but her memory had become suddenly sharp; she was broke these days, too.

So now he was rationed. He had half a package left, to be doled out one at a time only in emergencies.

He was on his third tonight.

Surrender now and you're free to go.

Rhan stared at the lit end, a fierce orange dot in the darkness. He'd had no choice but to kick in the Iceman's headlight. The guy was crazy! He couldn't be trusted. What you did, Rhan told himself, was self-defence.

Except it hadn't felt like that. Cornered in the glare of the Camaro's headlights, escape wasn't enough. He'd wanted to wipe the superior smirk off the Iceman's face and leave him with a mark of the battle so he'd never forget...

Brilliant pain. Rhan jumped, and dropped the cigarette. It had smouldered down and burnt his fingers. He picked up the butt and flicked it outside, his heart tripping.

This thing with the Iceman had to stop now, tonight. He couldn't get sucked into a fight he didn't want.

But what if he was already in it?

He doesn't know you, Rhan told himself. If you stay away from the arcade, he can't find you. He'll pick on somebody else, eventually.

He was more worried about himself, that he'd blown it again. He had to get back on track, concentrate on his training. He had to figure out how to control this thing.

The smallest tremor of doubt. What if he couldn't? What if the power was bigger than he could handle?

I'll give it up, Rhan thought bluntly. I'll give it up and just be...normal.

His stomach dropped, like the plunge down an elevator shaft. He hoped it wouldn't come to that.

FIVE

R HAN stood on the dresser in his room, the top of his head almost brushing the ceiling. He'd just hoisted the big straight-backed chair up with him and now he paused to catch his breath, still holding it. They didn't make chairs like this any more, he thought, a trickle of sweat snaking down his bare back. This sucker was solid. And it seemed more solid every time he hauled it up.

On the floor below him the four dresser drawers were set on their ends to get the most height, arranged like stepping stones from the bureau to the bed. Out in the world, Saturday morning cartoons were on. Rhan knew he was too old for cartoons but he loved them anyway. Self-sacrifice was the core of every training program.

He gulped a breath and stepped down. The drawer wobbled from the uneven weight, but Rhan shifted desperately to balance with his body. He walked from one drawer to the next until he reached the bed, then turned around and went back the same way. He could feel a hot band glowing across his shoulders and upper arms, but he drove himself on.

Okay, faster!

The route was second nature to him now; he'd been working at it most of the morning. He'd developed it for balance training and control, and

44

the awkward weight of the chair added a lesson in pain tolerance—good old Number Three. But he was doing it, dammit. He was doing it and every little step was something and one day he was going to *run* this gauntlet, blindfolded.

The thought spurred him. He tried a leap between drawers.

The extra force tipped the drawer out from under him. He hit the floor with a crash.

Rhan sat up dizzily. His steps were scattered and the chair lay toppled beside the dresser it had hit. Before he had time to stand up, the door to his room flew open. To his horror it was Zoe, in a bathrobe, her hair in a towel. She must have been in the shower, next to his room.

"What in God's name is going on in here?!"

Rhan's face was burning as he got quickly to his feet. "It was an experiment," he said defensively.

"An experiment? What kind of—" Zoe gave a sudden shriek and rushed over to the chair, hauling it upright.

"My chair! My beautiful antique Jacques and Hays straightback." Her voice dropped. "This was a gift."

Rhan felt a tug of conscience. It had looked like any old chair to him. He would have used a different one if he'd known it was special.

Zoe whirled on him. "First the police, now this! How dare you throw my furniture around? Who do you think you are?"

"And who do you think you are, busting in like that?" Rhan shot back. "You're the one with all the rules about doors. Maybe this is what I do when I *chant*."

Zoe's eyes flashed, but the noise had brought Gran. She puffed into the room and stopped, surveying the mess.

"Shirtless hell," she said.

Zoe put her hand on her hip. "This...*child* of yours has been calmly destroying my heirloom furniture."

"Look, it's not even scratched," Rhan started.

"I take you in—against my better judgement—and this is what I get for it? The privilege of having my home trashed by a destructive little thug?"

Gran stiffened. "I don't think a few drawers on the floor is 'trashed,'" she said. "And I wouldn't go around callin' names, if I were you. You're not exactly Miss Manners yourself. Last week this destructive little thug cleaned ten of the filthiest rugs I ever seen in my life and there was never a word of thank you."

"I'd say free room and board is a pretty fair thank you," Zoe snapped.

"And you wouldn't miss the chance to rub it in!"

Just then there was the sound of a buzzer, the one wired to the door of the motel's reception area. A customer.

A look of alarm crossed Zoe's face. She was

still wearing a robe and towel. "Well, could you get it?"

Gran folded her arms across her chest. For seconds the two women glared at each other, but finally the younger one broke down.

"Please."

Gran turned triumphantly and sauntered toward the stairs. Zoe seized the chair and huffed out. Rhan shut the door after her, with his foot.

It took awhile to put everything back. After he'd gotten dressed, he crept quietly downstairs to get his jacket out of the closet. He had his hand on the doorknob when Gran came out of the front office.

"I don't know what was going on in that room, but it sure as hell better be cleaned up now," she said in a low voice.

"It is."

"What did you need them for, all those drawers?"

"An experiment," Rhan said wearily.

"Well, I don't want to hear about any more of 'em. You gotta respect things that aren't yours. Zoe's right. We're in her house."

Rhan started to speak but she cut him off. "There's no two ways here. Zoe had good reason to blow her top." She paused, studying him. "This is kid stuff, you know."

Rhan turned the knob and pushed out.

The November wind stung his face and skittled brown leaves across his path. He crunched them under his feet, zigzagging to get them all. He didn't know where he was going and he didn't care.

That bag and her heirloom furniture. How was he supposed to know what was special and what wasn't?

But underneath, it was Gran who was troubling him. Defending him one minute, turning on him the next; he didn't understand it. They didn't seem to be able to talk to each other in that house, and there were things he was starting to need to know. It was frustrating when one person was your whole family.

Rhan's parents had been dead for ten years. There were pictures of his mother, a brown-eyed, fawn-haired woman with an uncertain smile, as if she wasn't sure you were going to like her, Rhan thought. He'd seen the same pictures so often they'd lost their realness. Like in magazine photos, the woman seemed human but distant, as unreachable as a movie star.

There was one picture of his father's left hand. He'd found it in Gran's drawer last year, a studio photograph of his mother sitting, the hand on her shoulder. It wasn't large but it was clearly a man's hand, knobby and long-fingered, with wisps of dark hair just before the blue shirt cuff. It had been severed at the wrist by a single snip. Gran couldn't have cut away more without slicing off her daughter's shoulder.

Rhan had stared at the picture, wondering if

Raymond Siske was left-handed, if he was looking at the part that had pulled the trigger, the part of the man capable of murder and suicide.

Gran had caught him, and she'd taken the picture away.

"It doesn't do any good," she'd said, but not unkindly. "I tell myself it's up to God to even the score. That's how I keep getting out of bed in the morning."

Walking down an unfamiliar street in Thunder Bay, Rhan wasn't thinking about the score. He was wondering how tall he could expect to be, how soon he could expect to shave, and who would ever teach him to drive.

He realized suddenly that he was freezing. Face, fingers, even his ears were growing numb. A new gust of wind made him grimace. The smell of money again. He had to get out of this, just for awhile.

There wasn't much nearby. On one side of the street there was a strip mall of offices. On the other side was a gas station and garage, called Gervais Automotive. The building had another sign that said Snak Mart, and he started for it. He could get a little something inside, and he could warm up.

Closer now, past the pumps and heading for the door, he saw one more sign, hand-lettered and stuck in the window with yellowing tape. *Help Wanted.*

No kidding, Rhan thought. Who'd want to be

a gas jockey in this frigid part of the country?

He pushed in through the door, and his glasses grew blurry from the instant warmth. When they cleared, he noticed the woman behind the till.

She was sitting on a high stool with her back to him, leaning on a shelf that was covered with paper. There was a phone on the shelf and she must have just dialled.

"Yes, this is Mrs. Gervais calling, from Gervais Automotive. I'd like to speak to your accounts department," she said crisply into the receiver.

Her hair came just past her shoulders, a glossy brown the colour of Hershey's chocolate, full of thick waves and curves.

Curls, he elbowed himself mentally, but it was an easy slip to make. Shoulders, arms, back— there were no harsh lines to this woman. Just round smooth surfaces, each easing into the next. He found his eyes following the taut seam of her blue jeans up and over her ample hips.

Jesus, Van! This is Mrs. somebody. Cut it out. He turned away guiltily to stare at a rack of magazines. But he couldn't stop listening, and in a few seconds he was stealing glances over the top of the rack.

"I'd like to bring to your attention several invoices which are overdue..." Mrs. Gervais said into the phone. "When we set up your account, we made clear our net thirty day policy..."

For half a minute there was silence as the other

person spoke.

"Yes, and I understand that," Mrs. Gervais said. "But like you, we must meet our obligations. Many of our suppliers are net *seven* days. Now, we do value your business, but I'm afraid I'll have to put your drivers on a cash-only basis unless I have the full balance by Tuesday morning..."

Rhan could almost hear the customer squirm. Mrs. Gervais, he thought, was one tough cookie.

"No, that won't be sufficient. I'll send a courier Tuesday morning to pick up the cheque. Could you have it waiting at the front desk by 9 A.M.? Good. Thank you very much."

She hung up the phone, made a notation and turned around.

"Oh!" She started with surprise. She hadn't known he was standing there.

But Rhan was surprised himself. He stared at the smooth pink-cheeked face and wide brown eyes barely touched by mascara. The brisk, determined bill-collector was no older than he was.

And she was fading fast. Like a flower folding in for the night, she seemed to curl up in front of him.

"What can I do for you?" she asked shyly.

"*You're* Mrs. Gervais?" he blurted.

Her hands flew to her cheeks and she flushed to the roots of her hair. "Oh, God, no! That's my mom. I just...help out sometimes."

Rhan could feel her embarrassment in the pit of his stomach.

"Well, you had *me* convinced," he said hurriedly. "I was ready to send the money. I think they could hire you out to the mob."

She laughed suddenly, clear and bright.

"Oh, I'm not that tough..."

"Are you kidding? He was shaking in his boots. I could hear his teeth rattle from here."

"Well, you have to let them know you mean business," she said. "It's not easy running a small shop. Lots of people keep from paying their bills as long as they can. Or they only pay whoever squawks."

"And you're pretty squawky."

It made her shrug and laugh again, but at the same time she seemed to realize they were face to face. Her eyes moved to the till.

"What can I do for you?" she repeated.

This girl had a way about her that made him want to step closer, listen harder. But he was already up against the counter and he could feel his time was running out. Buy something, do something!

"I was thinking about applying for the job," he said.

She smiled quickly and reached for the phone. "Let me get my dad."

A few seconds later the door that connected the Snak Mart to the garage swung open. The man who came in was short, compact and wiry; his rumpled coveralls were spotted with grease like a jungle camouflage. He was smoking a cigarette and had a toque perched uncertainly on the top of his head.

"Oh, Dad! Don't wear it like *that*. You look like a geek," the girl said, embarrassed again.

The mechanic looked delighted. "I love this hat," he said, but the curl in his voice told Rhan that he loved it all—the toque and the embarrassment and the girl.

He led Rhan through the service bays and toward a tiny office. The garage itself was high-ceilinged but narrow, with just enough space for three vehicles squeezed together. Another figure in coveralls was hunched over, almost into, a car's open hood.

While the mechanic shuffled through the papers on the desk in the office, looking for an application form, Rhan read the licence on the wall. Maurice Gervais, it said. The mechanic noticed him looking.

"Everybody who doesn't call me Dad calls me Moe," he said.

A voice rang out from the garage. "Gee, *Dad*, can I have a raise in my allowance?"

"Christ, Bernie, if you were my kid, I'd be in the old folks home by now," Moe called back.

"Coming sooner than you think, Moe," Bernie answered cheerfully.

Moe was looking for someone to pump gas on Saturdays and some weeknights.

"It's only minimum wage," he said, shrugging apologetically. "Makes it hard to get help, if all the mills are up and running. I can't compete with that."

Rhan thought of J.R. and the shiny black four-by-four. Even a grunt made more than minimum wage, he was sure.

"Hey, Moe," Bernie interrupted. "Come look at this."

The mechanic left the office and leaned over the open hood; amazingly, the toque didn't fall. When Bernie started the engine, Rhan lost their voices, but he followed their faces. Bernie was perplexed, Moe was intent. The older man reached into the engine, straining to turn some-thing deep inside. He adjusted and listened, then adjusted again.

Rhan stood in the doorway. He had never been anywhere like this. It was so vivid: the smell of grease and cigarettes, the cars and the toque and the bill collector. It seemed to wrap around him like a blanket.

The rugged roar was still vibrating the small shop, but Moe was walking back now, wiping his hands on a rag.

"So—you want to fill out an application?" he cried over the noise.

Rhan seized the oily hand and started shaking it. "Mr. Moe, I think I'll be the best pump atten-dant you ever had!"

SIX

RHAN went hurtling home with the news. "I got a job, I got a real job!"

It brought both women out into the living room.

"What kind of job?" Gran said.

"And where?" Zoe said.

"This is for money?" Gran said.

"You're not working for Tom Pauley, I hope," Zoe admonished. "The whole city knows the man is a crook."

When Rhan finally wriggled back into the conversation, he told them about Gervais Automotive. Gran's face went grim.

"Not a gas station. Gas stations get robbed."

"Everybody gets robbed," Zoe said. "*This* motel has been robbed."

"Every time people check out, judging by the towels," Gran muttered. Zoe shot her a look.

"I'm taking the job," Rhan cut in. "He offered it to me and I'm taking it."

Gran crossed her arms over her chest. "Well, now, mister, I don't think you are. You got enough in your day with school."

Rhan let go a short breath of disbelief. "Oh, come on. I've checked out my classes...this school is a joke!"

"You haven't given me nothing to laugh about lately."

"Look, I can keep up..."

"That's not good enough," Gran said angrily. "What about university? You won't get there by 'keeping up.'"

"Well, he's not going to get there without money," Zoe cut in.

"Maybe I don't want to get there at all," Rhan blurted.

The room fell silent. Gran's face looked flat, like a photograph. Rhan could feel the heat in his cheeks—him, who could lie without blinking. But he'd started now. He had to say it all.

"Maybe I'm tired of getting ready for my life. Maybe I just want to live it."

For a second no one spoke. Then Zoe looked at Gran.

"Lucy, I think anyone who hasn't made an educational decision yet should work at a gas station for awhile."

Gran became strangely calm.

"Zoe, girl, you're absolutely right."

Rhan was suspicious. "What?" he said.

Gran started toward the kitchen. "Now, I picked up some paint samples you oughta have a look at, for the front office. Cheapest redecorating there is, you know."

Zoe followed her. Rhan thought he saw the faint twitch of a smile.

"I start next Saturday," he called after them. But they were already in the kitchen, talking about shades of grey.

A week later Rhan was at the gas station early. He huddled in the doorway of the Snak Mart, trying to stay out of the wind. His toes and fingers were numb by the time he saw the Gervais minivan pull up at five to eight, but he felt a hopeful tug when four bundled figures jumped out. The whole family had come to the garage today.

"Left the dog at home, though," Moe said cheerfully. "*Somebody's* got to chew the carpet."

"Oh, she hasn't done it in months, Moe," Mrs. Gervais called, flicking on the lights. "She much prefers the taste of the couch!"

Rhan liked the real Mrs. Gervais instantly. A large, generous woman, she had a pixie cut of dark hair and a light spray of freckles. In her bulky parka and well-worn boots, she looked like someone ready to lend a hand, at anything.

Andrea—Andy—was the youngest daughter, and Rhan guessed she had gotten the genes of a distant relative. Nine or ten, she was long and stringy, with a blunt cut of wheat-coloured hair that framed her narrow face. She eyed Rhan as she pretended to sort the magazines.

The other daughter made coffee, although no one had asked. Rhan watched her deftly clean the old, sodden grounds out of the filter, then bundle up the overflowing garbage bag and haul it outside. If the bill-collector was shy, it wasn't of work.

"Me and Bernie are booked right solid today,"

Moe said, gesturing at the young woman. "Kate will teach you the ropes."

Kate. Rhan liked the sound of her name, even in his own head. He almost said it out loud, just to hear it again.

The Snak Mart was cheery now, warmed as much by the smell of fresh coffee as anything else. Moe filled his mug and headed for the garage door. "Three women and only fifteen minutes behind schedule. We're not doing half bad. Suit him up, Ann. We'd better get rolling."

Mrs. Gervais turned to Rhan. "Come on, love. Fashion calls," she said with a wink.

She led him to the back of the Snak Mart. Inside a storage room she unhooked a hanger with a full-length coverall uniform. The entire thing was bright red, except for the words embroidered in white over the breast pocket: "Ask me about Bonus Bucks!"

Rhan tugged on the suit while the women watched.

"How does it fit?" Mrs. Gervais asked, pulling the fabric across his shoulders.

Rhan took a few steps, listening to the swish, swish of the bulky suit. "Fine. I just feel like I should be directing something down a runway." Everyone laughed.

"You should see Katie in one," Andy piped up. "She looks like a red bowling ball."

"Andy!" Mrs. Gervais snapped. The girl shrugged and sauntered around to the magazine rack.

There were other red uniforms hanging in the closet, but Kate didn't put one on.

"I'll just wear my jacket today," she said, not looking at her mother, or Rhan.

When Mrs. Gervais brought out two plastic trays of money, Kate took one with both hands and leaned toward her mother.

"And would you keep the brat in here, please!" she whispered tersely.

Mrs. Gervais pursed her lips but didn't answer.

Rhan followed Kate out into the wind. She unlocked the small booth, then opened the cash register with another key. She turned on a small baseboard heater, which quickly glowed orange behind its metal grill. There was easily enough room for the two of them in the booth, but she edged over nervously until she was pressed against the windowed wall.

Her eyes on the cash register, Kate explained that his float would always contain one hundred dollars in small bills and change, but he could "buy" more from the Snak Mart if he ran short. She did a quick demonstration of the till, her fingers nimbly skipping over the code keys as well as the number keys as she rang up an imaginary sale. Then she voided it.

"At the end of today, I'll show you how to balance your cash report. We always start each person with a new float. That way, if the day's cash is short—"

"You know who's heading for the border," Rhan said.

She finally glanced at him and grinned for the first time.

A car pulled up to the pumps then and he followed her as she served: gas, windows, check the oil. He felt stupid just standing there, especially since Kate moved around the vehicle with confident ease. He had no experience with cars. When she hauled up the hood to check the car's oil level, he drifted in close.

"You were born to this, right? Gas nozzle in one hand, dipstick in the other? You've been doing this all your life."

"No, it just feels like it." Kate grimaced as she pushed the dipstick deep and wiggled it. For the first time Rhan noticed the delicate gold chain around her wrist, and the paper-thin heart that dangled from it.

The customer paid and Kate handed Rhan the twenty-dollar bill, telling him to try to ring it in. He hesitated in front of the unfamiliar register, then swiftly punched in the sequence of codes for the transaction. The drawer popped out and he gathered back the change. When he turned to Kate, her eyes were wide.

"Hey, you did it right!"

"Yeah...wasn't I supposed to?"

Kate was shaking her head. "When we first got that machine, it took my dad a *day* to learn the codes and what order to put them in."

Rhan was thinking of other codes, maze sequences he had to remember or be annihilated on the screen. Learn or die, he thought proudly.

"I have a good memory," he said.

But not for everything. Twice he forgot to hand back Bonus Bucks, the coupons customers got on their gas purchase. And one woman seemed in such a hurry that he didn't bother to ask about the oil.

After that car had pulled away, Kate tapped the metal sign beside the pumps.

We promise...
to clean your windshield
offer to check your oil
give Bonus Bucks on your purchase
or
WE'LL GIVE YOU $10 IN BONUS BUCKS...FREE

"Always," Kate said. "We always have to remember. Believe me, there are people just waiting for you to make a mistake. And that costs us money."

But the morning was warming up. After awhile the wind eased and the sun broke through the clouds in patches. Kate watched him from the booth and it made him glad that he was getting good enough to solo. When there was a lull in business, he asked questions.

Work answers she was good with: credit-card purchases and what brands of oil had the biggest profit margin. When he asked what school she went to, he was surprised it was McKay.

"Really? I started there two weeks ago but I don't remember seeing you."

"Oh, you wouldn't," Kate said hurriedly. "I kind of blend in. I'm not somebody you'd remember."

"Are you kidding?" Rhan said. "Like I'd forget Mafia Telemarketing? The call you can't refuse?"

It took her a second to realize he was joking, and then she laughed. She looked surprised.

At noon Kate suggested they go into the Snak Mart.

"I should really give my mom a break on the till. She and Dad like to get away for lunch. You could eat at the front counter—that's what I always do. You can watch the pumps through the window, in case somebody comes."

Only Andy was in the Snak Mart.

"Where's Mom?" Kate asked, stepping behind the counter.

"Talking to Dad." Andy popped a cheese twist into her mouth. Kate noticed the bag in her sister's hand.

"Hey, did you pay for that?"

"Yes."

"Liar. You're always taking things without paying. I'm telling mom."

"Go ahead and tell, bossy—I don't care," Andy shot back. "You're just jealous anyway because you can't have any. You're on a *diet*."

Kate flushed scarlet. "I am not!"

"Yes, you are! You've been on a diet all week because of *him*!" Her finger shot out at Rhan with obvious delight. "You said he was *cute*."

Kate's hands were curled into fists on the front counter. She could barely get the words out. "You...little...witch!"

"Katie's on a di-et, Katie's on a di-et," Andy sang.

Kate looked like she might fly across the counter at her sister. Instead she rushed past Rhan and through the door to the garage.

Rhan stood, stunned. He could just make out Kate's voice beyond the door. He didn't know what she was saying but he could hear the tears. Andy smirked at him, then munched another cheese twist.

A horn blared. Rhan whipped around, banging into the edge of the counter as he struggled to open the door and get out. After he'd served and the car had driven away, he sat down on the stool in the booth. He wasn't hungry any more.

What *was* that? he wondered. Why hadn't Kate fought back? That's what he would have done. Or faked it. You never let your opponent see you sweat. Everybody knew that.

There had to be something else going on here, something he didn't understand. Sisters—like cars—were outside his range of experience.

And he couldn't understand why Kate would be on a diet anyway. She wasn't fat, she was...cushy. He liked that. She looked, he realized, like someone you could hug.

The desire caught him by surprise, a warm flicker that was part memory and part hope. He didn't have much experience at being close, but he wanted to be near this girl.

The real hazard was him. Rhan knew he charged into things; he could overwhelm people. It had taken the bill collector most of the morning to laugh out loud.

Just be nice, Van. Be calm and don't rush it.

But he could feel the change of things, under his coveralls and his jacket and his clothes. He wondered if she'd really said he was cute.

At four o'clock Moe ambled out to the booth. He was carrying a new float of change.

"Well, that's it for you today. How'd it go?"

"Good," Rhan said, lifting his own tray out of the till. "Great."

Moe settled onto the stool, looking tired and rumpled. "My next shift doesn't show up till six," he explained, rubbing the back of his neck.

Rhan hesitated, the tray in his hands. "Uh...Kate said she'd show me how to do the cash report." The question was in his voice.

The mechanic looked at him for a long moment, and Rhan felt uneasy. Moe had to know what had happened at lunch. Was he mad about it? And could a father look into your face and know what you'd been thinking about his daughter?

"Well, you take it to her, then," Moe said finally. "She's in the office. You tell her I said she's the only one who could show you properly."

"Okay." Rhan felt a rush of gratitude and relief.

"And check the schedule...I've got you down Wednesday six to nine, plus Saturday."

"Okay."

"And, hey!"

Rhan, already steps away, swung around.

"I hear you've got these bloody codes figured out already," Moe said, his weary face lighting up. "Good for you. I need an expert around here."

Rhan felt light once he'd taken off the bulky coveralls, but chilled, too. The red suit was warm. He passed through the empty garage, still carrying the tray of money. He guessed that Bernie had gone home.

The door to Moe's office was closed. Rhan took a breath before he knocked. Slow, he reminded himself.

"What?" Kate's voice was muffled, miserable.

"It's me," he said to the door. "Rhan. Your dad said you're the best one to show me the cash report."

For seconds there was no sound. What if she refused? He didn't want to go home without seeing her but he didn't want to push it, either.

There was a soft shuffling noise, and then Kate let him in, turning quickly away. She cleared the desk—it looked as if she'd been working with ledgers—and pulled out sheets labelled Daily

65

Cash Report. Rhan pulled up a chair as close as he dared and Kate briskly explained each column, keeping her eyes on the paper. What little Rhan could see of her face looked parched, dried out.

"Then," Kate finished, "you count out the float and put it back in the tray, and wrap up the rest of the money like this." She folded the report around the bills. "Put it in the bank bag and give it to my mom or dad, whoever's here. They do the deposit every night. Got it?"

"Got it," Rhan said, but he didn't move. Kate hesitated, looking uncomfortable. Then she began pulling the ledgers out again.

"Okay," she said stiffly. "I have to get back to work."

"I'm sorry," Rhan said.

For a moment she seemed to freeze. "You don't have anything to be sorry about," she said.

"I know. But somebody's got to be and I figure this time it'll be me. Next time it could be somebody else."

Kate was holding a pencil, like a bridge between her hands, rolling it over and over. "You're not from here, are you?" she asked softly.

Rhan was puzzled. She knew where he'd moved from.

"I mean, you're not shy," Kate continued, a note of wonder in her voice. "I've trained three guys on the pumps and none of them ever really *talked* to me. It's like they were embarrassed that a girl was showing them how to pump gas. But today was different, not like working at all. It was *fun*..."

"I'm more fun on a date," Rhan blurted.

The room was very quiet, so quiet he could hear the cash register in the Snak Mart. He hurried on nervously, trying to fill the empty air. "We could do anything you want. A movie, anything. I mean, that's only if you *want* to and...and if you don't mind waiting. I have to wait until your dad pays me. And," he felt a real twinge, "I don't have a car or anything."

She had stopped rolling the pencil, and now she was just holding it. Rhan's heart was in his mouth. So much for slow. Jesus, Van! Can't you ever make a decision and not—

"I have a car," Kate said finally, and she smiled. "And I just got paid, too."

SEVEN

"WELL, this is sort of sudden, isn't it?" Gran said, standing in the doorway to his room. Rhan was irritated. It seemed to him that she'd knocked and opened in the same moment. He was fresh out of the shower and wearing only sweatpants, dripping on the floor while he looked for his comb. He felt a lot less than half dressed.

"What do you mean, sudden? I said do you want to go to a movie with me and she said yes. It's hard to drag that out."

"I mean, what kind of girl would go on a date on such short notice?"

"One with *taste*," Rhan said. He pulled open the dresser's top drawer and rummaged noisily.

"You just met her."

"No, I met her before. And we worked together all day."

"What kind of girl works at a gas station?"

"An heiress!" Rhan snapped. "Her dad *owns* the place." He turned around and noticed the comb in the back pocket of his jeans, which were laid over the end of the bed. He stalked over and whipped it out, not meeting his grandmother's eyes.

"The boss's daughter," Gran said gravely. "I don't know if that's such a good idea. And you're

68

rushing it, maybe. You don't want to make the same mistake twice."

Rhan froze. "What's that supposed to mean?"

"It means you didn't spend a lot of time getting references on that last girl you fell for. And we both know that didn't come up roses."

"Jesus Christ!" Rhan pitched the comb at the open drawer but it struck the edge and skittered across the floor. "Okay, so I made some mistakes. But this is different. This is somebody completely different!"

Gran looked at the comb on the floor, then back at him.

"And you're still the same. You fall too fast, mister. And that's a danger."

She pulled the door shut as she left. Rhan dropped onto the bed. He guessed it was too late to try to borrow some money.

Fifteen minutes later he was standing outside the Trail's End waiting for Kate to pull up in her car. Every breath was a puff of frost, and his still-damp hair was stiffening in the cold. But he didn't want her to come to the door.

His day with the Gervais family seemed like a dream. He ran it over in his mind, savouring it—even the fight, even the dog he'd never seen. That was how real families worked, Rhan thought. Kate wasn't ready for Gran and Zoe yet. Or the rest of it. There were parts of his life that he'd tell her eventually, but for tonight he'd avoid them. It wasn't lying if you just kept the truth out of sight.

When Kate's Dodge Plymouth pulled into the lot, he opened the passenger door before she'd come to a full stop.

"Hi," he said.

"You should have told me it was this place," Kate said. "I drive past here all the time but I never knew the street address. I was looking for a house."

"It's a test," Rhan said quickly. "It's how I weed out the poor navigators."

Kate laughed. "Then I'm done for. I can do my own tune-ups but I can't find my way out of a mall parking lot. Speaking of which," she said, steering the Plymouth onto the main road, "how about the Cineplex at UniCity? We'll have six movies to choose from."

Rhan didn't answer. He'd been avoiding UniCity since that Friday night. He'd avoided the arcade and the mall and the streets around it. He wasn't afraid, he'd just...decided. He was being careful.

But it's been a week, Rhan thought. A week and a day. That was long enough to forget, wasn't it?

And how could he refuse if she was buying? He didn't want to screw this up.

"Rhan?" Kate said.

"Left at the lights, Captain, then full speed ahead."

Kate kept her eyes on the road, but he noticed her smiling to herself. She liked, he thought, being called Captain.

Away from the garage and other people, Kate seemed more at ease, and Rhan was relieved. No matter what he'd told Gran, the date *had* come together fast. He hadn't known what to expect. Would she be shy or sorry or what? But Kate had the ability to surprise him. The girl behind the wheel seemed like someone new—nervous but bold at the same time.

Rhan caught himself staring shamelessly. He liked the way her glossy brown hair fell against her evergreen jacket. There was a shadow of pink on her cheeks and a fragrance around her that reminded him of a forest. It made him wonder. Men could be clean or less clean; they could wear old clothes or new. But girls, Rhan thought, had some other ability, a way to magnify everything you liked in the first place.

"Do you live at the Trail's End or are you just staying there until your family finds a place?" Kate asked.

It jarred him to hear the word "family." This was the stuff he'd been hoping to avoid. But he didn't know any way around it.

"I live with my gran and her cousin Zoe, who's the owner," Rhan said.

Kate was silent, as if she was waiting for more. When it didn't come, she continued on, a little nervously.

"Then you're like us," she said. "A family business. Do you enjoy it?"

What was to enjoy? Rhan wondered. Cleaning

filthy carpets? Listening to the washing machine chug twenty-four hours a day?

"Sure," he said.

"Me, too," Kate said. "But it's frustrating sometimes, because we all work so hard and it seems like there's no way you can win. Like now. We're in this big fight with a credit-card company. Dad got a phone order for a re-built carburetor, with a credit-card number. He got authorization on the card so he shipped the carburetor. But now the credit company says they won't honour the purchase because the guy was way over his limit and we don't have a signed slip! We were on the phone with them all last week, battling it out. It's been a nightmare."

Rhan shook his head. Carburetors and credit cards—that *would* be a nightmare. He couldn't imagine spending an hour on the problem, never mind a week.

"Do you ever think about doing something else?" he asked. "Like for a career?"

Kate glanced at him a little shyly. "After I graduate, I want to go through to be a CGA."

"Branch of the FBI?"

"No, it stands for Certified General Accountant."

"Accountant!" Rhan couldn't keep the laughter out of his voice. "Why that?"

"Well, to be free."

Rhan fell silent, surprised.

"Look at it this way," Kate said. "My dad's a

good mechanic—he's a great mechanic—but he figures that as long as people keep coming through the door, business is fine. He should be able to do what he wants."

"Like what?"

"Like building an extra bay on the garage."

"Your dad wants to add another bay?"

"No, he already did," Kate said angrily, "and it just about sank him."

Construction had to be financed and then another mechanic hired, she explained. All the expenses—wages, interest—had to be paid whether more customers came in or not.

"Why do you think I help out on the books so much? Because my mom has to work the late shift at CP three nights a week so we can pay the loan on the bay that was supposed to bring in so much extra money!"

Kate stopped herself and took a deep breath. She loosened her grip on the steering wheel, but her eyes were still fixed on the road in front of her.

"I love my dad," she said after a moment. "But he's a doer, not a planner. And you can't win like that. Good accounting will get you the answers *before* you sell your soul to the bank. If you can plan for what you want, you're safe. You're free."

Rhan's head was spinning. The outburst had taken him completely by surprise, like this girl, like this whole day. He felt a tug of awe, and envy. Kate knew what she was going to do, she knew why, and she knew how. All he had was four generalities on a scrap of paper—a shopping list.

"I think you'll be a great CGA," Rhan said. "The best. The Gretzky of accounting. The banks will tremble."

Kate shrugged, embarrassed. "Oh, don't. Talking about it is the easy part. It's just something I'd like to do."

Rhan liked sitting beside her in the dark theatre. Perfume and popcorn, and his shoulder growing warm against hers. He kept his face toward the screen but he watched the lights flicker against the silhouette of her left leg.

Gran was wrong. This wasn't dangerous. Today he'd felt the safest he could remember. He wasn't haunted by his list, he didn't worry about anyone getting hurt. Learning the pumps and being with Kate had been the whole glorious day.

He took Kate's hand suddenly, as if he was afraid she'd get up and leave.

"You're not shy, are you?" she whispered.

"I'm not from here," Rhan whispered back.

Walking out into the mall again, into the bright lights and crush of people, Kate let go. Rhan blinked himself awake, alert. He was glad that the mall exit was nearby.

"Do you want to get a coffee or something?" Kate asked.

"Sure. Where?"

Kate checked her watch. "Well, we can still get

to the food court. They stay open later than the stores."

Rhan felt a twitch of nerves. The food court was within sight of the arcade. But then he was mad at himself. Careful didn't mean cowardly, for God's sake. He couldn't change his whole *life*.

Nearing the tables, Kate faltered.

"What?" Rhan said.

"It's two friends of mine, Patrice and Lindsay."

He heard the tension in her voice, although he couldn't understand it.

"We could go somewhere else," he said hopefully.

Just at that moment, one of the distant girls waved.

"No, it's...it's okay. Here." Kate tugged him behind a cluster of shoppers and thrust money into his hand. "You buy. And don't give me the change."

Before he could answer, she slipped out of the crowd and started toward her friends, smiling brightly.

Lindsay was the one who had waved, a gangly girl with dark straight hair and a perpetual giggle. Patrice was as slender as a sapling, with ash blonde, over-permed hair and gold hoop earrings that touched her shoulders. Lindsay invited them to sit down and Patrice gave him a long, appraising glance.

"So you're the one," she said.

"Right," Rhan said. The one for *what*?

"We heard a lot about you this week," Patrice said.

"A lot," Lindsay repeated, giggling.

"Where'd you get a name like Rhan?" Patrice said.

For an instant he was stunned. He hadn't been introduced yet. He glanced at Kate, who looked stricken. That was enough for him. Whatever game was going on here, he was ready to play.

"From K-Tel," Rhan said, looking Patrice dead in the eye. "Only $9.95. It slices, it dices—and I can use it as a verb."

There was a second's silence before the girls laughed uneasily. But Patrice was still up to bat.

"It was one of those seventies leftovers, right? Like Chastity or Moon Unit? I bet the get-up came with it free," she said, gesturing at his clothes. "Don't worry, the drug-dealer look is always in—in certain society."

Rhan straightened. "Well, you know your crowd better than I do—"

"Look!" Kate cut in suddenly, desperately. "Isn't that Tracy Hammond with Jeff Turcott?"

Patrice and Lindsay swivelled, as if on cue. Kate sent Rhan a pleading glance. He was irritated. He was just warming up.

But the distraction did the trick; the Hammond-Turcott item was hot gossip. Kate seemed relieved that they weren't talking about her date any more, and she seized on the new sub-

76

ject with nervous energy. Rhan's gaze drifted toward the arcade.

The longing swept him up; he flexed his fingers unconsciously. In his mind's eye the little knight of Gemini Planet was still where he'd left him, trapped in the earth within sight of the door. He had a wild urge to set him free.

But Captain John's was closing now, the players being herded out reluctantly.

Rhan sat up. In the swirl of bodies around the arcade, he thought he saw someone. For an instant the eyes in the distant face seemed to catch his. His heart kicked over. He leaned, straining for a better view. The face was gone, blended into the crowd, but he couldn't stop looking. Was it? And if it was, then what?

The silence made him realize something was wrong. He turned to the three girls, who were staring up at him. He was standing.

"Leaving so soon?" Patrice said drily.

Kate jumped up, too.

"I...I think we'd better. It's getting late."

They walked through the emptying mall, Kate with her hands in her jacket pockets, her eyes on the shiny floor in front of her. Rhan glanced over his shoulder, but only four or five stragglers were in front of the arcade.

"I'm sorry my friends gave you a hard time," Kate said quietly. "They don't really mean it. Maybe I should have warned you about Patrice."

Rhan snorted. "Miss Congeniality?"

"Well, she's outspoken. That's what I like about her. I'm just sorry she turned it on you."

"She was doing it to you," Rhan said.

Kate coloured. "Oh, no. She's my best friend. Anyway," she continued quickly, "she's probably just intimidated because you're from Vancouver."

Rhan stopped. "Wait a minute. How would she know that? And how did she know my name? You didn't even find out until today."

Kate was blushing furiously now. "Well, it was on your application..."

"You saw that?"

"Just a peek, real fast. Don't be mad—I just had to find out who you were."

She looked fearful but Rhan laughed suddenly, relieved. It struck him as a compliment.

"Did you do a credit check, too?"

Kate grinned. "You're clear," she said.

The night had turned around again. Heading for the exit, they walked so close that their shoulders almost touched. He and Kate seemed to do better, Rhan thought, the farther away they got from other people. Underneath, he was filled with amazement that anyone had wanted to know about him that badly. Coming from Kate, a credit check was...romantic.

As soon as Rhan pushed out through the mall doors, they both stopped. There was an inch of snow on the ground and it was still falling; the dark sky seemed to be in motion and blurry white halos surrounded the parking-lot lamps. Rhan had been dreading the snow, knew he'd hate it with all his heart, but the big flakes piling up so softly on the cars and asphalt caught him unprepared. It was perfect. Magic.

Kate knew it, too. "Now I have an excuse if I can't find the car," she said dreamily.

"Aye, aye, Captain. Navigator to the rescue," Rhan said, and he took her hand as if he'd done it a hundred times, not once in the dark. He led her through the lot, teasing her that she'd parked in another province, but inside marvelling at the heat of her hand and the blue-white glitter all around them and how easily it all fit together...

Wham! The pain burst in his left shoulder blade, wrenched him from Kate and threw him hands-first into the snow. For a second he was too stunned to think, but the freezing slush up his sleeves brought him around fast. In revulsion he started to get up.

"Don't move."

The voice knifed through him. Oh, God! In a single, panicked reflex he flipped over. The thick end of a baseball bat slammed the ground beside him, warning him.

Kate gave a startled cry, like a scream cut off before it ever had a chance.

EIGHT

RHAN was on his back, propped up on his elbows, his pounding heart hurtling the blood through his veins. At first all he could focus on was the blunt end of the bat, pointing straight at him. But he forced his gaze up the wooden shaft, up the long arm to the Iceman's face. The glittering eyes were a strange contrast against the hard, pale surface of his skin—living lights set into a statue.

"Tell her not to make that noise again."

At the very edge of his vision, Rhan could see Kate rooted in the snow, her hands to her mouth as if the cry had surprised her, too. Was she out of swinging range? Why didn't she run?

The abrupt jab of the bat toward his face made Rhan flinch and squirm back into the snow already melting under him.

"*Please* tell her."

"Don't scream, Kate." *Run*, for Christ's sake!

She was already thinking of it. But at the faintest movement of her foot in the snow, the Iceman's free arm shot out to point at her.

"She'd better stay here. In case you have an accident."

Kate froze and Rhan felt the stranglehold of frustration. He couldn't risk anything if Kate wasn't safely out of the way.

Which was exactly what the Iceman had planned.

"Behold, Descent begins—and ground becomes your prison." He smiled faintly. "Don't worry, this won't take long."

The Iceman withdrew the bat and rested on it like a walking stick. He crouched cautiously and scooped something out of the snow, his eyes never leaving Rhan. From this new angle Rhan could see an ugly raw scrape along the Iceman's right cheekbone. Whatever fights he'd been in this week, he hadn't won them all.

Then he noticed what his adversary had picked up out of the snow—a hardball. What if the thing had hit him in the head?

"You could have killed me!"

"If I was trying to, sure. But I wasn't. Not yet, anyway."

"Who are you? What do you want?" Kate blurted.

The Iceman didn't look at her. "She's so concerned. It's almost touching. That must be why you chose her. She certainly wasn't the best looking of the three."

So it *had* been him at the mall! But Rhan couldn't allow the slur to pass; he moved to get up. In a blur of grey the bat was in his face again, forcing him back miserably into the wet, freezing slush.

"What do you want?" he croaked.

"Only my due." The Iceman didn't withdraw

the weapon but tucked the ball into his jacket pocket and held out his hand. "Your glasses, please."

"What?"

"You heard me. *Now*."

Rhan thought the fury would choke him, but what could he do? He pulled off his glasses and handed them over, feeling new panic as he peered up at the blurred face of his assailant. How was he going to win if he couldn't see?

"I think you know the rules. An eye for an eye..." The Iceman dropped the glasses near his foot and ground down on one of the lenses with his heel. The dull crack was barely audible, but Kate gasped and Rhan winced. His glasses cost money—money he didn't have!

"I don't forget, amateur, if that's what you were thinking. But I can forgive, so here's another chance. Surrender now and it's all over. You'll never see me again. Just say the magic words."

The silence stretched. Rhan's tongue was against his teeth but he wouldn't speak.

"Rhan," Kate pleaded.

The name did it. The Iceman glanced at her for the first time. Rhan seized the moment and flipped over, a wild roll to get out of the way. The thick end of the bat came down beside him and Rhan booted at it desperately, knocking it out of the Iceman's grip. It spun away over the slippery parking lot but not out of range. The Iceman lunged for it. Already up on one knee, Rhan dove to intercept. His shoulder hit ribs...

*...the knight was running across the barren land-
scape, the panels in his armour brilliant with the full
power of Ascent. A sudden arrow out of nowhere shot
toward him like a missile, striking his breastplate in
a shower of sparks. The knight stumbled but didn't
fall. Now the archer appeared on a small rise. He fit-
ted another arrow into the bow. Still running, the
knight drew his sword and swung it over his head
with a cry. There was a streak of silver before the
arrow pierced his wrist...*

Rhan flinched, and realized he was in a parking lot. What the hell had just happened? An
arm's length away, the Iceman was sprawled out
in the snow, too. This close, Rhan could see his
startled face. He looked young, and curiously
frightened. As if he'd seen a ghost.

Rhan rolled and scrambled to his feet. He was out
of swinging range by the time the Iceman scooped
the bat out of the snow. This was their chance!
Unguarded, Kate made a break for the mall. Rhan
turned to bolt after her, but he'd only taken a few
steps when the voice rang out behind him.

"Retreat is surrender—and I accept."

Rhan stopped, as if he'd run into a knife. He
spun around.

"I never surrender!"

"Really?" The Iceman slung the bat over his
shoulder. "I'm still on the screen, aren't I? I gave
you a week. You'd *better* sit with the girls, amateur. There's no place on the field of honour for a
coward."

The word twisted the blade, gouged him in a place he didn't even know he had. Rhan took a step, every nerve awake and roaring.

"Prepare, Iceman!"

The call rang over the parking lot; distant shoppers turned to look. Rhan's eyes were fastened on his opponent, as if he could force him into focus by an act of will. But the blurred face was unreadable. The Iceman began to saunter away.

Rhan finally turned to go after Kate, but she hadn't made it to the mall. She was standing, staring at him as if she suddenly didn't know who he was.

◆

O, valiant warrior, we've long awaited your arrival!

Rhan knew exactly where he was. His grandmother had a handful of ways to say it, and he'd heard them all. Between a rock and a hard place. When push comes to shove. Caught between the devil and the deep blue sea.

Our benevolent ruler has been overpowered by his evil twin and now serves the forces of darkness.

Rhan didn't know the face of the benevolent twin; he didn't know if the overpowered ruler was still living or not. It didn't matter.

Because he'd seen the forces of darkness. He'd seen it in a man who would attack an unarmed opponent, who would terrify an innocent girl.

It was a cold, silent ride back to the Trail's

End. The heat in the car was on but Rhan's wet clothes were still clammy punishment. His broken glasses were in his jacket pocket, the frame bent and one lens gone. His left shoulder throbbed, but that was nothing compared to the truth grinding through him. He'd made a mistake. A big one.

He hadn't thought the Iceman would forget, just that he'd let it go. That's how it worked, didn't it? Once you proved you would push back, it was over. Rhan thought of that intent face, those brilliant eyes drilling into him. He knew now that if he hadn't shown up at the mall, the Iceman would have gone looking for him. Thunder Bay wasn't big enough to lose him. He didn't know if any city was big enough.

He wouldn't underestimate this guy again. You made a mistake and you paid for it, Rhan thought. Learn or die, RanVan.

His chest tightened. In his mind's eye he saw a flash, the silver streak of an arrow. He didn't understand what had happened when he'd collided with the Iceman, the burst of vivid images, as if a dream had exploded inside his head. He knew he had a good imagination, but this was different. Like a movie, if you could feel it, too. It worried him. And he already had lots to be worried about.

"It wasn't random, was it?" Kate said suddenly. "You know him, or he knows you."

Her voice startled him. He'd almost forgotten she was there.

85

"Not...not really. I've only seen him a couple of times, at the arcade. I guess he figures I insulted him." It wasn't a complete lie but not exactly the truth, either.

The old Plymouth bounced up over the sloped curb and into the Trail's End parking lot. Kate put the car in neutral and it sat, idling softly.

"They're a bad bunch at the arcade. Dealers, everything. I guess you didn't know—you just got here. But none of my friends hang around there. I would have warned you, if I'd met you before." Kate took a deep breath. "We've got to go to the police."

Rhan tensed. "No, we don't."

"Yes, we do. The guy is a psychopath! He threatened you with a weapon, he threatened me. We can't just pretend nothing happened."

They weren't the first to be attacked at the mall, Kate said. There had been one incident after another. A year ago, a fourteen-year-old skateboarding in the parking lot had been beaten so badly with his own skateboard that he was in the hospital for four months.

"There wasn't even a reason for it. These guys just went after him," Kate said angrily. "It was all over the papers. I mean, he was just a kid and he almost died."

She stared at the car's dark hood through the steering wheel. "This isn't the U.S. or Toronto. It's *Thunder Bay*. Where do you have to live so you can have a normal life? So you're not afraid?"

His heart was in his mouth. He didn't want Kate to be afraid—ever. He wanted to tell her he was a knight and he was trying to be finished as fast as he could. But he wouldn't risk that. He'd already learned the hard way: people thought he was crazy when he told them the truth.

And there could be no police. This was between him and the Iceman.

"Look, if we drag the cops into this, everybody's going to get upset—your mom and dad, my gran." *Especially* Gran, he thought. "And how are they going to find him? I don't even know the guy's name."

Kate looked at him sharply. "You called him Iceman. That must mean something."

"It's...it's just a code name he plays under. At the arcade."

"Well, they can look for him there, then. That's not our problem."

"No, our problem is when he gets a suspended sentence and comes up to bat with a grudge!"

Her eyes widened, hurt. Rhan was instantly sorry he'd raised his voice. He shifted, edging just a bit closer, wishing he could touch her, take her hand again. But he couldn't. They weren't the same people who'd started this date.

"You don't have anything to be afraid of," he said. "It's not you he's after. I swear, you'll never see him again."

"But you will. That's what you told him—to get ready." Her voice twisted in frustration. "I don't understand men. They all think they have something to prove. And it's just so crazy, it's so violent. I really thought you were different."

Tell her. Tell her now.

"I like you so much," Rhan said. And he did. This bill collector whose little sister could make her cry, this Gretzky accountant with the bad sense of direction. He'd been wanting to hug her since morning.

For a minute there was only the smooth sound of the Plymouth's engine.

"I have to think about this," Kate whispered. "Please go now."

"Kate—"

"Please."

He got out of the car. He drifted around to the driver's side, reluctant to leave, his wet clothes already beginning to stiffen in the wind. When he saw her wipe at her eyes with the heel of her palm, the pain was sudden and swift. He stepped up to the window and touched the glass.

The movement made her flinch. She thrust the car into gear and hit the gas, the wheels spraying back snow until they caught a piece of pavement.

Rhan watched until even the bright red of her tail lights had disappeared.

NINE

THE lights were out in the main office when Rhan let himself in quietly with his key. Most motels kept their offices open until midnight, but the Trail's End wasn't most motels. Old people went to bed early. Rhan leaned against the wall to take off his runners, and the touch of something solid almost collapsed him. For awhile he just stayed there, alone in the dark, fighting for breath.

There was the flare of a match in the living room. Rhan straightened, self-conscious. He peered at the dim room and after a second he made out the blurred shape of Zoe sitting in the big ratty armchair. The last person in the world he wanted to see.

Just make it to your room, he told himself.

A second later the pungent smell wafted over. American cigarettes! The scent of his old favourites was almost painful. He'd never needed one more. Rhan found himself standing next to the armchair, still in his jacket.

"You got an extra?" he said. His ragged voice surprised him.

It surprised Zoe, too. She hesitated, then held out the package. Kingsize! Rhan sat on the arm of the nearby couch and lit up hungrily.

"I keep quitting," Zoe said, "and then I have a crisis."

For the first time Rhan noticed her face, how pale and washed out it was. She looked like he felt.

"What about all that serenity?" Rhan said.

"Tibetan monks don't have to deal with women."

It was an odd thing to hear from a woman. He thought about Kate and Andy in the Snak Mart, and Kate's two friends in the mall. With men, at least the battle lines were clear.

"How come you and Gran hate each other?" he asked.

"Well, I wouldn't say *hate*," Zoe said.

"Okay. How come you can't stand each other?"

"How about we don't *under*stand each other?" Zoe said.

"Okay."

Zoe puffed on her cigarette and exhaled thoughtfully. "I went to live in a women's commune, in the seventies."

"So?"

"I don't think Lucy agreed with the lifestyle. We were into a lot of... alternatives. You know, herbal medicine, meditation, healing through visualization..."

"Chanting?"

Zoe smiled faintly. "Chanting."

"So what's the big deal?" Rhan said, puzzled. "I mean, she reads the *National Enquirer*."

Zoe hesitated, studying him. "Our group was a chapter of Wicca. White witches."

Rhan's first impulse was to laugh—he was smoking Marlboros with a bonafide schizo. But a strange thought ran through him. He didn't tell people he was a knight for the same reasons. Because they would laugh, because they would think he was nuts.

He took a cautious drag. "So you put a hex on Gran and pissed her off?"

Zoe shook her head with disgust. "You people. You interpret without knowing anything. Wicca means 'wise woman'—witches were the first doctors, you know. Our group studied the ancient techniques of healing, and how to focus positive energy...for *positive* results. We didn't hex anybody." She leaned forward. "Look, witches aren't special or different. We're just interested in learning how to use the powers the Creator gave *all* of us."

Rhan felt a strike inside him. "What kind of powers?"

"Well, the natural ones. Regeneration, ESP, precognition..."

"Did you ever have a dream while you were awake?"

The night seemed to stop. Zoe looked at him. "Why?"

"I...I just want to know."

The longest pause. "Some of us used to practise scrying."

"What's that?"

"You'd know it as crystal gazing, but people

use anything—a mirror, a pan of water. Anything you can stare at that gets you into a state of deeply relaxed concentration and lets your subconscious project images, the way it does when you dream. I knew a woman who said she could scry while watching daytime soaps."

"What about you?" Rhan said.

"I used to use a mirror."

"Used to? You don't do it any more?"

Zoe shook her head.

"Well, how come?" Rhan prodded, impatient. This was like pulling teeth.

"I had a...dream that a woman died. And then she did." Zoe took a breath. "It was your mom."

Rhan felt pressed into the arm of the sofa, frozen to it. Out in the street a truck rumbled by.

"You know, if you're interested, I've got some good books," Zoe said finally, changing the subject. She got out of the chair and started toward a small bookshelf.

Rhan pushed himself up and stabbed the cigarette in the ashtray.

"Thanks for the smoke," he said abruptly. He jogged up the stairs, trying not to look like he was running.

You're okay, he told himself. It's weird but it doesn't have anything to do with you.

That night Rhan dreamed he had to move in with the Gervais family. The reason was vague and menacing and nameless—he just showed up at the door, rain-soaked and scared. He kept glancing over his shoulder.

Would they let him in? What would he tell them? How could he ever explain this?

When Mrs. Gervais opened the door, he only got out one word. "Please..." he blurted.

"We've been waiting for you, love," she said with a wink. "I held dinner."

Stumbling into the warm house, Rhan almost melted with relief. But in seconds the succulent smell of something roasting in the oven turned him inside out. He was hungry—worse than hungry. He was starving. From the den came the happy rise and fall of the TV. Someone was winning a hockey game.

"Send him in when he's fixed up, Ann," Moe called over the roar. "Vancouver's having a hell of a second period."

"Katie, you take him downstairs and get him out of those wet clothes," Mrs. Gervais said.

On the dim staircase, Kate caught his hand in a sudden squeeze. The heat sent a ray of hope up from his knees.

"My dad likes you so much," she said. The world was fading away behind them, one step at a time.

There was a pull-out couch already made up with care—sheets and pillows and blankets, the cover turned down expectantly.

"This is where you'll sleep," Kate said. She sat down and waited.

The dim light, the abundant curves, she

smelled like a forest. He was trembling—worse than hungry. Ravenous.

"Please," he whispered.

Kate took his hand one more time.

She gasped when he squeezed her. He loved the sound in his ear, and the cushy softness of her against him. Rhan closed his eyes. He didn't need to see how beautiful she was. He knew with his hands and his lips, he knew with every inch of his skin...

He woke with a shock of joy, and then disappointment, and then disgust.

It's only a dream, Van.

But some dreams you weren't the same after. Rhan was haunted. He might be a knight, but parts of him were really, really mortal. He got up wearily and began stripping the sheets.

It snowed and snowed. After its brief moment Saturday night, the snow was no longer pretty. Sanded with gravel, or ploughed up into banks along the streets, it turned grey and dismal. Sunday afternoon Rhan and Gran struggled out by bus to a distant mall that had a one-hour eyeglass shop.

Gran was mad, especially since he wouldn't tell her what had happened.

"They just broke. I'm sorry," Rhan said woodenly.

"Well, how? They fly off and get run over by a car? This girl must have slapped your face pretty hard."

Rhan opened his mouth to protest, then shut it. If she had it all figured out anyway, he wasn't even going to talk.

What really bothered her, though, was that she'd had to borrow the money from Zoe.

"We're just gettin' in deeper and deeper," Gran said with a sigh. "Like digging a hole you'll never get out of. Some days I wonder if I got the strength to keep on trying."

She sounded so tired. Rhan thought of the endless loads of laundry and all the painting she'd done in the front office. She'd cleaned two check-outs this morning. Zoe knew slave labour when she saw it.

"I'm the one who's paying her back," he snapped. "Don't let her wring it out of you. And anyway, we could have done this tomorrow. After school."

"No, we couldn't. I already got...plans." Gran looked out the window. "Tomorrow's enough of a day as it is."

Rhan would have asked why, but he suddenly remembered he wasn't talking. He folded his arms over his chest and let the bus carry him along.

TEN

H E went to school Monday determined to get answers. There were things he had to find out: who the Iceman really was, where he went to school, where he lived. The personalized licence plate was something people would remember, something they'd know him by. But he had to be careful; he didn't want to alert the Iceman's friends.

Class after class he found a way to pull some-body aside and mention the white Camaro. Lots of people had seen it but nobody could name the driver.

"Probably from Port Arthur," he heard, over and over, as if the other half of the city was the Great Unknown. Didn't these people ever walk across the street?

But he was under surveillance, too. In his three weeks at McKay he'd never noticed Patrice and Lindsay before. Now they seemed to cross his path often, giggling, whispering, smirking.

"Hey, K-Tel man, what are you today—a noun or a verb?"

Heads turned but Rhan kept walking. Patrice couldn't irritate him, he decided. She was beneath his contempt.

J.R. tracked him down before lunch. "Saw some guy in a red suit on the weekend," he said pleasantly, falling into stride.

"Santa Claus," Rhan said.

"Santa's pumping gas now?"

"Has to. The elves went union and he's looking at two hundred years of back pay. And Mrs. Claus said she'll see him in court."

J.R. grinned. "Like seriously, how long you been working there?"

"Since Saturday."

"You should have asked me first, bud," J.R. said, a note of reproach in his voice. "There's a waiting list at CP, but hey, I know people. They always need sweepers."

Rhan sighed inwardly. He was already in a bad mood but J.R. had the ability to aggravate it.

"What's done is done, I guess," J.R. continued. "And anyway, I saw your assistant. Fringe benefits make up for the pay, right? She looks like an armful, too, for a little guy like you."

The flick of pain, like the snap from a wet towel. Rhan felt his hands curl into fists but he fought the urge, picked up speed and pulled away.

"Well, see you," J.R. called cheerfully.

It's just the way he is, Rhan told himself. He's not smart enough to be mean.

He saw Kate once, at her locker. He stopped in his tracks and just watched her stack books on the top shelf, unable to take his eyes off the slight swing of her hair, the robust curve of her behind.

His day at the garage rushed back at him, and the dream. Just to be funny for someone, Rhan thought. Just to listen and talk and be there and touch.... He didn't care if people liked him. But a person—singular, female, possessive—he could care about that. A lot.

Rhan forced himself to turn around and start walking. She'd said she had to think about him, and that was okay. Because he had something to deal with, too.

◆

"Come on, *ladies*, ten minutes! Show me some hustle!" Mr. Rosner barked. But they had been hustling for forty minutes already—lay-ups and running drills, a thunder of basketballs ringing through the gym. Now that Rosner had divided them into teams for a last quick game, the fire was sporadic. It was the last class of the day, and everybody was counting down the seconds to the bell.

Rhan couldn't get excited about team sports. He was nimble enough if he got the ball, but when the bulky guys got up to speed, they mowed him down; Rosner was real casual about fouls. And for what? To put a ball through a lousy hoop? The prize wasn't big enough, Rhan decided.

But Rosner was quick to flail them for not trying. Rhan worked hard to look better than he was. The guy he was supposed to be guarding was a moose with elbows. Rhan shadowed him dutifully but let him get *just* out of reach when he turned snarly. Illusion, he thought, would get him through basketball.

Thud! The gym floor came up fast. His moose bolted down the court and buried the ball, to a ragged cheer.

Rhan pulled himself up, in time for the shove.

"Van, you cockroach—you were supposed to be guarding him!"

He reached for a retort but there was nothing. The buzzer vibrated through the gym.

"Last one out, put the balls away!" Rosner called over the stampede for the door. Rhan's teammate scooped up a ball and fired it at him, hard.

He let them all troop out, lingering as he gathered the balls into laundry baskets. So what if it was the end of the day? There wasn't anything to hurry home to.

He was on his way to the showers when he passed a door, and stopped. It was the weight room. The air around him was silent, only the faint echo of people passing by in the hall outside. Rhan let the little room draw him in.

Stuffy. Worse than the locker room. The stench of sweat seemed to waft out of the walls. He touched the unfamiliar equipment, ran his hand over the cool metal. When he saw that the barbell on the floor was stacked for 160 pounds, his chest tightened.

Something had been bothering him since Saturday night. Why hadn't he transformed in the parking lot? The power was his. Shouldn't he be able to turn it on when he needed it?

1. Perfect existing skills.

Rhan stood over the bar. He knew how this should go. He'd watched it on TV.

He positioned his feet slightly wider than his shoulders and dropped into a squat, gripping the bar one hand over, one hand under.

Okay, just stand up. Stand...up.

He felt the strain in his hip joints, then his thighs. He gritted his teeth and forced himself straight, pressure tightening to pain that leapt to include his shoulders. The side that had taken the baseball was howling, and he heard his breath coming in gasps. But he was standing!

Okay, jerk it to your chest and get underneath. Then push up.

His body was crying out for release. Every second the bar seemed to get heavier. He hated his hesitation and the way he was shaking.

Come on, *cockroach.*

With a gust of fury he jerked the bar, but it never made it to his chest. Midway everything was gone and he was powerless to stop the drop. The metal rang dully on the concrete. Not loud, but loud enough.

◆

"Hey, little bud!"

Rhan kept walking toward the exit. The thought of being anybody's little bud made his stomach roll, but he knew why this guy was on his heels. It was that damn suite he wanted. He had

100

to develop J.R. repellent, and soon.

"How's it going?" J.R. said, catching up.

"It's gone, thanks," Rhan said. "But the doctor gave me some cream in case it comes back."

J.R. hit the lockers when he got it.

"Whoa, are you *gross*, Van!" he chortled. "I've gotta use that one some time."

Rhan shook his head in disbelief. Did nothing work on this guy?

"Hey, listen. I forgot to tell you—I'm having this party at my place, Saturday. My parents are going Christmas shopping in T.O., so it'll be a real hoot. You can bring somebody if you want, but there'll be lots to choose from."

"I don't know. I might be working," Rhan said. Actually, he was sure of it, no matter what.

"Well, you could come after. Anyhow, it's ten bucks a head for beer, at the door."

They pushed through the exit at the same time, into the school parking lot. Rhan shuddered at the blast of cold air, but he was relieved. Almost free.

"You want a ride home?" J.R. asked.

"No, it's okay, thanks," Rhan said, veering off sharply.

"Okay, but check when you work. And don't forget! Ten bucks and we'll save you a few on ice."

The word twigged on Rhan. He swivelled suddenly.

"Hey, J.R.! Do you know who drives a white Camaro with the licence plate ICEMAN?"

For long seconds the lanky young man just

stood there, silent. Rhan began to feel uneasy. He'd been so careful, but what if he'd blundered into the wrong guy? Maybe J.R. was a friend...

"What's he done now?" J.R. said finally.

Rhan took the ride.

The Iceman's real name was Lee Dahl, and J.R. didn't just know him, he was related. Cousins, he also worked with Lee's older brother, Reine, at the mill.

"Reine's full time, though, a unit manager. My uncle buggered off six years ago, left my Aunt Helen with both kids. It was real tough until Reine went to work. He's twenty-three now but he lives at home, just about supports the whole family. The guy's a saint," J.R. finished, shaking his head.

"What about...Lee?" Rhan said.

J.R. snorted. His cousin was in grade eleven at Gordon Draft—when he felt like it. He'd never had a job. In the past two years he'd been charged twice: theft under $500 and three counts of damage under $1000.

"Breaking windshields," J.R. explained, "but that's just what he's been caught at. If it was me, I would have thrown the asshole out. So what does Reine do? Buys him the car! Is that reverse psychology or what? Reine's not stupid. The Camaro's in his name. He can pull it any time, if he has to."

Rhan felt dizzy at his good luck. He'd hit a nerve and he'd listen as long as he could get J.R. to talk.

"What's the licence plate mean?" he asked, although he thought he'd figured it out. He remembered an Iceman as one of the superheroes in Marvel Comics' X-Men.

"The Canadian 3-D Championship, two years ago," J.R. said.

"What—those little cards where the picture comes out at you?"

J.R. looked at him sideways. Lee, Rhan learned, was an archer, and a pretty good one. Good enough to place in the top twenty when he was fifteen.

"Bow hunters come from all over Canada for the championship. He was the youngest guy to place in the money. He used to shoot just recurve—you know, a traditional bow—at jamborees and stuff. But he got into the compound bow and that was it."

"Bow hunter," Rhan repeated. He felt as if he'd collided with a ghost.

"Well, they don't actually kill anything at the competition. They just go along this roped-off trail and shoot at targets, these styrofoam deer. But you only get one shot at each target. I guess he was real cool, incredible. The guy who covered it for *The Marksman* called him that. Iceman."

The championship was Lee's last competition. Rhan wanted to know if he was still shooting.

"I don't know," J.R. said bluntly. "You can't talk to the guy—he goes strange on you." His voice lowered. "We're at this family barbecue, on

103

Labour Day, right? I figure I'll go over and talk to the guy. Be nice. I say How's it goin' and he says, 'Did you know that Heracles killed his kids in a fit of madness—and he was demi-god?' Jesus!"

A week after that, Lee shaved his head.

"You know, *bald*? That just about put Aunt Helen in an institution. She was phoning my mom every day."

That explained it, Rhan thought. The sense of the skull. The Iceman's hair wasn't short, it was new.

J.R. was thinking. "So what do you want him for, *really*?"

When he'd first gotten into the truck, Rhan had said he'd been talking to the Iceman about buying the white Camaro, but he'd lost the phone number. Now he realized how transparent the lie was to anyone who knew Lee Dahl.

"He tried to run me down in a parking lot," Rhan said.

J.R. sucked in a breath and let it out slowly, but he didn't look surprised.

"I wouldn't say this about somebody else. Hell, I'd help you pitch the guy...if it was somebody else." He shook his head. "Let it go, bud. He comes after you again, go to the cops. Otherwise, you're better off to just stay out of his way."

Rhan stared out over the truck's black hood. He couldn't tell J.R. that "again" had happened, and that they were already standing in each other's way.

The four-by-four pulled into the Trail's End parking lot. It was snowing now, big flakes melting against the warm windshield. Rhan saw J.R. looking at the suites.

"Thanks for the ride," Rhan said, grabbing the door handle.

"Any time. Hey, about that key..."

Rhan felt something snap. It was time to end this, here and now.

"I can't," he said abruptly. "The keys are always locked up and we're always booked anyway and...I just can't."

J.R.'s grin fell, but then he shrugged.

"Can't blame a man for trying," he said. "Catch you later," he called as Rhan got out of the truck.

Rhan didn't say goodbye. He strode through the fresh snow toward the motel, trying to stay ahead of the uneasiness on his heels. *So he's an archer. So it's another coincidence. Tell it to Stephen King.*

Rhan carefully slid a map out of the front office drawer and took the phone book out of the kitchen. He carried them both up to his room, under his jacket.

ELEVEN

"WHERE do you think you're going?" Gran said.

Rhan stopped, feeling caught. He was wearing a T-shirt, a sweatshirt, a kangaroo jacket with a hood, his jean jacket and his new ski gloves.

"To take a shower," he said irritably.

"Well, bring a shovel with you."

"What?"

"You heard me. That parking lot needs doing and there's still an hour till supper."

"Maybe I already have plans," Rhan started.

"And maybe you just changed them."

He let out an exasperated sigh. "Come on. She's got a service..."

"And it costs her money every time she calls them out," Gran said.

"So why should I care? It's not our place, is it?"

Gran drew herself up, blue eyes glittering. "Let's get something straight right *now*, fella. While we're here, this motel is our business, too. It puts a roof over your head, it puts a roof over mine. Not to mention this lady just lent you the money to replace a pair of glasses you weren't smart enough to keep on your face."

"I'm paying her back, all right? She knows that!"

"We're talking effort, not just money. Between the laundry and the upkeep, there's enough work here for five people. I don't know who you think you are these days, but if you're not ready to give a hand—without backtalk—you can march your self-centred little butt right out that door." Her voice dropped. "You shame me."

Rhan's face was scalding. He turned abruptly and headed out, past the open door of the office where Zoe stood, eyes wide.

He went to get a shovel out of the little shed that stood beside the house, almost even with the front office. No more than a lean-to, it was windowless with a flat, slanted roof. Rhan left the door open behind him, but shuffling around in the cluttered darkness, he whammed his foot against a pile of debris on the floor.

The jolt brought water to his eyes and he swore out loud. He hauled the armload of junk outside and threw it down alongside the shed wall. In the yard light he could make out what he must have hit: a lead pipe, mottled with rust, as long as his arm. He stared at it grimly.

3. Pain. Why did he keep getting the same damn lesson over and over?

He seized the shovel and dug in. The lot was enormous, a white ocean. He knew it was impossible to do in a single night, but he wasn't about to go back. Let them drag him in at midnight. Then they'd be sorry.

Tire tracks made him curse; the weight of the

cars had packed the snow stubbornly. Rhan threw his anger behind the blade and the chunks flew left and right.

But he couldn't seem to chip away that word. Shame.

Damn it, Rhan thought. Damn it anyway. Why was she being so hard on him all of a sudden? What had gotten into her? Okay, so he hadn't been the nicest guy in the world lately, but he was a knight, for Christ's sake! He had other things to worry about. If only she knew how hard he was trying to—

To what, Van? To track down a guy so you can beat him?

His own conscience caught him cold. When he thought of it like that, it wasn't a knight's purpose at all. He was the Defender—he was supposed to help people. Tracking down Lee Dahl was as far from helping as he could get.

But what am I supposed to do? he wondered, chiseling at another tire track. Just stand here and wait for it?

In that instant he realized he nearly believed in it—that arrow coming straight for him. And he knew that the sick knot in his stomach was fear.

Rhan stopped and leaned on the handle, trembling. Come on, Van. So the old witch tells spooky stories. This is real life, and you're in charge of what you believe.

He started to work again, more slowly. The only way to get through this is to take control of the situation, he told himself. Go meet it in the light of day. He hoisted a heavy load of snow. And in the meantime, try not to be such a jerk.

Twilight deepened to black sky. He discovered that it was easier to push the snow than lift it, and he settled into a routine of scraping long straight paths to the edge of the parking lot, where he piled a running bank. Still, his muscles burned; he felt the supper hour come and go.

Rhan didn't know what time it was when he stood, panting lightly, looking out at the clear lot with pride and disbelief. He was exhausted but somehow he'd finished—the impossible had been done.

Inside the house his dinner waited in a glass container, ready for the microwave. But he was too grubby and tired. All he wanted was a long, hot shower and his bed. He'd just made it to the top of the stairs when he heard his name.

Rhan turned wearily. A red and white rectangle came whizzing up at him. He caught it, a reflex, and stared in amazement at the fresh package of Marlboros. American—kingsize!

"Good job," Zoe said.

The guy who was trying to not be such a jerk hesitated.

"Any time," he said at last.

◆

Tuesday morning was bright and sunny. Rhan went to school feeling better. The Iceman wasn't a ghost—he had an address. There had been five Dahls in the phone book but 826 Sifton was the only listing between Gordon Draft and UniCity Mall.

He knew there were things he should be worrying about, like a plan. But he could feel the anticipation powering up inside him, the pull to go there, to see. The Iceman had surprised him twice, but now it was his turn.

A few times he had to rein himself in. This wasn't revenge. Under no circumstances was this revenge. All he wanted to do with Lee Dahl was ...impress him. Scare him away so it would be over.

But he felt a twist of excitement, like the moment you stopped in front of a game, the money in your hand.

The final bell went at 3:20. By 3:21 Rhan was pulling on his jacket, tugging on his gloves. He had a few pages of homework—question sheets—but he folded them into quarters and stuffed them in his back pocket. He was travelling light.

He'd memorized the eight blocks to Sifton Street, home of R. Dahl. The last two blocks were the hardest, the streets rising in an unrelenting slope. Worse, this part of the city hadn't been sanded yet and some patches were treacherous; he had no boots. Crossing the last intersection he slipped and almost fell, catching himself at the last second.

Okay, he thought, the alarm still thumping under his jacket. Be impressive *without* traction.

Number 826 Sifton was unremarkable, and Rhan was relieved. A stucco bi-level, it looked dingy against the fresh cover of snow on the lawn. The blue shutters were peeling; windblown ad flyers clung to the iron railing around the doorstep.

But there were no cars parked in the drive. He didn't know if the Iceman lived here or not. Rhan started across the street for a closer look. Maybe the back yard would tell him something.

As soon as he touched the sidewalk in front of the house, it was as if he'd hit an invisible trip-wire. A blur of gold burst out of a faded doghouse in the back yard and headed straight for him. Rhan stumbled back in panic but the dog reached the end of its chain halfway onto the front lawn. It leapt and jumped, raging with noise.

A noise he'd never heard before. Rhan stared in horror at the golden Labrador retriever that yelped at him with a frantic, squeaky cough like a rusty gate. Was the animal choking? How could it be choking and keep jumping?

Rhan couldn't stand it any longer. He crossed the road again and to his relief, the dog fell silent. But it stayed in the yard, watching him intently. Rhan couldn't stop looking at its glossy coat and enormous brown eyes. Quiet, it was beautiful, a perfect Lab. Rhan felt his chest tighten. He didn't know anything about dogs, but he knew that

111

something had happened to this one. An accident, or injustice.

Just then, the Lab looked to its left. Rhan heard the dim sound of an engine and looked, too. The white Camaro was two blocks away, chugging up the street toward him. Rhan ducked into the closest yard with a high fence. Hardly noble, but he wasn't ready yet. The dog had thrown him.

He listened until the engine cut, then peered out between a gap in the boards. The car had pulled up in front of 826 and parked on the street. Expressionless, Lee Dahl swung out and headed for the house.

Rhan's heart was racing. The skull and the familiar profile were a shock of memory, even in daylight. The thing he hadn't come here for—under any circumstances—was awake and pulsing.

"Shh, Chelsey. Jesus!"

The dog was lunging and squeaking at Lee as he came up the walk. The pathetic sound hit Rhan fresh: an accident or injustice. He knew this man was capable of both. He hated him all over again.

And then the Iceman dropped suddenly to one knee in the snow and threw his arms around the dog. She was an excited tremor of gold as she struggled to lick his face, but it was buried in her fur. On a front lawn, in broad daylight.

Finally Lee pulled away, rubbing Chelsey's head and neck a few times before he stood up. He glanced around like a thief, then unhooked the

Lab's collar from the chain. The faint words barely made it across the street.

"...a few minutes. He'll kill..."

The dog glanced once at the high fence of 827 Sifton, then followed her master eagerly into the house.

Rhan stood in the snow.

It doesn't change anything, he told himself. It doesn't undo what he did to you. And everybody's a hero to his dog.

Still he stood, cold and getting colder every second.

Look, you're here, he told himself. You came to give him the message, so do it. You don't have to hurt anything.

But how? His eyes caught on the white Camaro clinging tentatively to its spot on the tilted street.

Rhan hurried over to the car, one eye on the bi-level's front window. He grabbed the door handle, expecting it to be locked, but the catch let go with a click. Eyes never leaving the house, he swung into the driver's seat, the door ajar and one foot in the road. He fumbled for the emergency brake and finally closed his hand on it. Push or pull? He tried both until he heard the muffled clunk as it released. He hesitated—was he moving? But the car was still; in his imagination it seemed to hover. He withdrew carefully.

Okay, now the hard part.

Rhan hurried up the walk. The vanquished

had to see the face of the victor or it didn't count. He leaned on the bell, then dashed back to the road, poised in front of the Camaro's hood.

Seconds stretched and Rhan felt the clutch of nerves. What if Lee wasn't alone? What if it was Reine who answered the door, or the mother? What if he let Chelsey out first?

Then the inner door opened and Lee's face was behind the screen. Now or never.

"Looks like the planet's shifting again, *Lee*!"

Rhan threw himself at the car's front and heaved with all his might. The Camaro began to roll, slowly at first, then picking up speed. Rhan let go and stepped away, gasping. Lee burst through the screen door and stopped. He looked wildly from Rhan to the car, then Rhan, then the car.

"Shiiitt!"

Lee Dahl leapt halfway across the lawn in a single bound. He whipped past Rhan and into the road. The sight of the Iceman sprinting through the snow—in his socks—was pretty glorious.

For a second. Rhan's own stupidity came at him in a sickening bolt. The Camaro was heading directly for the icy intersection. The cars couldn't stop, even if they saw it in time. Somebody could hit it, somebody could get hurt—or worse. Oh, God, he'd never meant for that to happen!

But the Iceman was barrelling flat out, closing the gap between himself and the car. Rhan could see he was already starting to reach for the door handle. The idiot! He'd never make it inside to the brakes. The car could drag him to his death.

The power caught Rhan from behind, swept him up in its blue lightning and hurled him forward. If there was ground under his feet, he didn't feel it. He was electrified with a single thought. He couldn't halt the sliding car, only deflect it.

Think fast.

The Camaro was only ten yards from the intersection when Lee got his grip on the door handle. Two strides back, RanVan felt his guts clench. He was going to have to tackle him—to hell with the car. But in the next instant the Iceman wrenched open the door and, in a leap of stunning agility, he twisted around and inside. The precision was eerie, inhuman. But there was no time to be amazed.

"Right!" RanVan screamed. He vaulted forward and threw his full force at the front left side of the car, praying the Iceman knew what he meant.

He did. The wheels were turned when the impact came, forcing the car to skid off course in a wide arc until the back tires bumped the far curb. Just then a drycleaning truck rumbled through the intersection, barely six feet from where the Camaro rested sideways in the road.

The driver's door opened and the Iceman stood, his fingers curled around the top of the open door. Surprise had wiped his face clean of the superior smirk. Astonished, he looked almost noble.

But Rhan was wrestling with his own wonder. The leap had been...impossible.

"Warrior?" Lee said.

The word was out before Rhan could stop it. "Knight."

The Iceman nodded, as if to himself.

"That's it. That's what I saw." Pause. "Right through the wrist."

RanVan the victor began to back away; he stumbled and almost fell. Then he turned and bolted from the field of honour.

TWELVE

3. In what country were the first cave paintings discovered? Who is credited with the discovery?

Together the brothers are invincible. Their magic holds sway over the planet and its inhabitants.

4. What impact did the find have upon the study of anthropology?

Our world is in chaos.

The blare of a horn made Rhan jump. He dropped the question sheets beside the cash register and hastily pulled on his gloves as he backed out of the booth into the cold.

"It's about time," the man in the pick-up truck grumbled. "Gimme a fill. Super." Rhan hurried to the pumps, glancing toward the Snak Mart over the truck bed. Moe himself was on cash tonight. He hoped his boss hadn't heard the horn.

Rhan set the pump for automatic fill and then hustled back to clean the windshield. He hated the fact that he had to struggle to reach across the glass with the squeegee—trucks were so damn high—and the fact that he had an audience. Why couldn't people spend the time counting their money or something?

The driver had left his window unrolled.

"So that's what you do in there," he said, tilting his head at the booth. "Catch up on your sleep?"

"Homework," Rhan said shortly, but it was barely the truth. He hadn't made any progress on his question sheets—the same ones he was already late with and in trouble over. He hadn't been able to concentrate last night. Or since.

"Well, don't strain your brain," the driver said as Rhan handed back the change and the bonus bucks.

Rhan knew he was beyond strained. He felt stretched to breaking, one part of him running for his life and the other standing absolutely still.

When the truck was gone, he settled back inside the booth and picked up the sheets again. It didn't matter. He kept living through the same sixty seconds, from the horrible moment the Camaro began to roll.

I didn't mean it, he told himself. It was just...stupid.

Dangerously stupid. Deathly stupid. Somebody could have been killed. And any excuse he had was microscopic next to that.

Rhan felt sick. His mistakes were getting bigger and coming faster. And even if the Iceman didn't cause them, he... accelerated them. Part of Rhan wanted to throw down this battle here and now—and run.

But he couldn't.

"That's what I saw. Right through the wrist."

Rhan was shaken. Somehow Lee Dahl had

seen it, too, that waking dream in the parking lot. What did it all mean? What if the Iceman was...somebody? Like a knight.

No. Rhan curled the battered question sheets into a tight tube. The Iceman's twisted leap behind the wheel had been unlikely, but not magic. Split-second timing and a big shot of luck.

He's not like you, Rhan told himself. But the question was fierce and insistent. What was he dealing with here?

He was glad when his shift was over. The lonely booth seemed eerie at night. But as he pulled out his cash tray and locked the glass door, he felt nervous. Moe had been busy with a customer when Rhan had shown up for his shift. He'd barely glanced in his direction. Now Rhan wondered if Kate had told her father anything about their date. She'd been so upset, so determined to go to the police. He remembered her profile in the driver's window as she left. He had no experience with fathers, but he guessed how it would be if a certain guy had made your daughter cry, twice.

Rhan slunk into the Snak Mart. Moe was at the till, scowling in the smoke that trailed up from the cigarette in his mouth. The mechanic looked downright sinister as he studied a sheet of paper in his hand. Probably my separation slip, Rhan thought. Walking papers. As he hung up his red suit in the storage room, Moe let go a bitter string of curses.

Rhan picked up his tray and started for the

office to do his cash report. He was glad to get out of sight.

"Hey!"

Rhan froze. *I'm sorry! I never meant to hurt her. It was a mistake, an accident, I swear...*

"Do you know how to turn this damn thing off for the day?" Moe asked wearily, jerking his thumb at the cash register.

The sheet of paper, Rhan discovered, was actually a set of instruction codes to finalize the day's transactions and give a total, from both the pumps and the Snak Mart.

"Progress," Moe said with a snort. "I hate this sucker."

Rhan scanned the sheet as he positioned himself in front of the keyboard. "Looks like they've got this set up for a third on-line till," he said. "You've just got two, right? This one and the booth?"

Moe nodded.

"Okay, let's try this," Rhan muttered to himself as he punched at the keys. "It's function, access, total one...function, access, total two...function, three, *void*...total!" He hit the last key with a decisive snap. There was a second's silence. Then the machine rolled into a rhythmic whirring and clunking, spitting up the print-out of the day's transactions. Pay off!

Moe grinned, creasing his stubbly cheeks. "Good work. I would've been here till midnight."

Rhan basked in the praise. "Well, you said it.

You hired an expert."

"But not at everything."

For a moment there was only the sound of the register grinding out its numbers.

"But not at everything," Rhan agreed.

"You in some trouble?" Moe said. There was no threat in his voice, only concern. A parent's voice. He was so close that Rhan could smell the oil and the cigarette smoke, and another distant scent—sweat scrubbed away by industrial soap. No one in his house smelled like this, he realized with a pang.

Rhan shrugged.

"Katie doesn't have any brothers." Moe sighed. "She doesn't know...what it's like."

"Sometimes you can't back down," Rhan said.

Moe looked at him. Then his arm went up so suddenly that Rhan flinched, but the mechanic was reaching into his mouth. He pulled out a row of three teeth, from the upper right side, and set them on the counter.

"Green Briar Pub, 1982. I couldn't back down, either," Moe said, lisping slightly.

Rhan stared at the false teeth, perfect and white, and a faint chill went over him. He couldn't imagine Kate's dad fighting in a bar. Moe scooped up the bridgework and replaced it deftly.

"Listen. The other guy is always coming after the guy he thinks you are. If you surprise him, step away and be somebody else, he's going to hit air. You've always got the choice," Moe said quietly. "You're a smart kid. You can learn it faster than me."

Rhan felt Moe's hand on his shoulder, a friendly shake. "Now you better cash out. The missus gets off work at ten and if I'm not there to pick her up, she'll have my hide."

There was no irritation in his voice, only that other sound, easy and warm, like when Kate had been making fun of his toque. If Moe had a temper, it wasn't for his family.

In ten minutes Rhan was out in the cold again, head down, hurrying home. He didn't understand about stepping away from himself, didn't know what it meant to hit air. But he couldn't get over what it had been like, just for a second, wishing he was Moe's smart kid.

"Sorry I'm late. I had a little car trouble."

Rhan stopped in his tracks halfway across the parking lot of the Trail's End. Desperately he scanned the shed and house and cabins. The single yard light was on, and the spotlight over the wooden Trail's End sign. But there were still so many shadows, too many dark corners in which to hide.

The faintest movement, between the first and second cabins. The light caught on two pale surfaces—Lee's face and the bat slung over his shoulder.

Rhan's heart was running. "Look, I'll call the cops..." he started.

"Okay. I'll race you to the door."

Rhan knew he'd never make it. The startled

young man of yesterday was gone. The Iceman was back, and this time he had his boots on.

But he might beat him to the shed, on the other side of the house. In his mind's eye Rhan saw the pipe in the tumble of boards, remembered its solid, dull weight. If he could make it to the shed and scoop it out of the snow...

It'll be the most dangerously stupid thing you ever did.

"Come on, *knight*. There's only two choices: surrender or fight." Lee unslung the bat and took a step.

Choices. The spark of an idea—a hunch. Rhan exploded off the mark and went hurtling toward the shed. He saw a blur in his left eye, Lee moving to intercept, and he didn't look again.

Don't miss, just don't miss...

Two strides to the shed and then he leapt, grabbing for the lip of the low roof. He swung himself up desperately, hooked his knee over and rolled into the snow. He flipped onto his feet again just as Lee came up.

"I already knew you were fast, coward."

"You're the one who wanted a race," Rhan shot back. "So come on, let's go."

He turned toward the small outcrop that was the roof of the verandah-turned-office. He backed up as far as he dared, praying that the motel's old washing machine was chugging away and the TV was turned up—loud. Then he took a breath and charged.

He landed on his stomach in the unbroken snow, a cold shock on every strip of exposed skin. But he'd made it!

The Iceman was staring up in surprise, but he was still hanging onto his weapon.

"Take your time," Rhan said, panting a little. "I don't care if I win by a little or a lot."

"Win what?" Lee demanded, but Rhan could hear the curiosity.

"Did I mention you have to touch the chimney? That's the line." He saw the challenge sink in. Lee moved toward the shed, but when he realized he couldn't climb up holding the bat, he stopped.

Damn! Get motivational.

"Default is surrender—and I accept."

That did it. Lee threw down the bat and jumped, pulling himself nimbly onto the shed roof. He didn't wait but made the vault, a leap of such height and agility that Rhan scrambled to his side of the roof. This wasn't a spectator sport.

The top half of the house had looked promising from the ground. Two large windows, evenly spaced, and then a smaller one, above and between them. That was the attic window, set into the part of the wall where the roof sloped up into a point. Rhan grabbed at the framework of the window on his side and stepped onto the sill.

A minute later he was splayed out like a spider, one foot on top of the large window frame and the other on the inch-wide sill of the attic window.

He was clinging to woodwork, but he'd have to let go to move up. He realized if he let go of anything he could fall.

He was afraid his pounding heart would shake him off the wall, but he dared to turn his head. The Iceman was pulling himself onto the roof.

That did it. Rhan pushed off the attic window in a sudden, desperate jump. The fragile frame splintered under his foot, but he got his chest and shoulders onto the roof. He wriggled the rest of him up, dazed and drained.

There wasn't a second to lose. The Iceman was halfway to the chimney, moving cautiously, bent so that one hand trailed along the roof for balance. He glanced back at Rhan and then lunged for the goal.

A different kind of power burst inside Rhan—this jackass wasn't going to win! Weightless, he vaulted forward three strides before he hurled himself across a small drift at the chimney.

For a moment he just lay there, peering through his snowy glasses at the grip his black ski gloves had on the chimney. He'd won! But the rush of triumph was short-lived. He felt the shadow and flipped over onto his side. The vanquished was towering over him.

"Fickle Hera smiles on you—today," Lee said, grinning faintly. He turned and started down the slope, on the side nearest the shed. Rhan pulled himself to his feet. He was already lightheaded with exhaustion and the height. The roof of Zoe's house didn't feel like any place on earth.

"What are you?" he blurted.

Lee was carefully negotiating his way around a wind-crusted drift of snow. "The same as you. Just another mortal that the gods are jerking around."

"What?"

Lee turned. He looked pleased.

"They used to do this all the time. Boost their favourites or zap a bolt of lightning at whoever pissed them off. It's their entertainment."

"Whose entertainment?"

"The gods. Zeus, Hera, Apollo, Pallas Athene...all of them."

The names registered dimly with Rhan. "Greek stuff? Mythology?"

"Mythology," Lee repeated. "I wish." His gaze became intent. "What do *you* think you are?"

The stare made Rhan uneasy. The Iceman knew anyway, from yesterday.

"Knight, warrior," Lee said. "The title doesn't matter. You're a player, that's all. You're a bit of light on some celestial screen." He smiled grimly. "The video game of the gods."

"Oh, get real!" Rhan's fervour surprised him. "That's myth, for Christ's sake. Those people...that stuff didn't happen."

"Didn't it? They've dug up the city of Troy. It's real. Agamemnon was a real king. His death mask sits in a museum. Ten years ago, a man named Tim Severin made the same voyage as Jason and the Argonauts—and the landmarks were all there," Lee said triumphantly. "Millions of people around the world believe in other legends with less proof than that—and they get civic holidays for them, too."

The Iceman was having a good time, as if he had been waiting to have this argument. Rhan felt bewildered and unarmed—he hadn't read about any of this stuff.

"Okay, so maybe these stories were based on real places and some real people. So what? That doesn't have anything to do with me."

Lee cocked his head. "So tell me, what's the technique for pushing a car around? Or better yet, show me again."

A weak spot. Rhan was pretty sure he couldn't turn on the burst of strength he'd need for it. The weights at school had proved it to him. It wasn't a skill he'd perfected yet.

"The gods reward the bold and punish the fearful," Lee said quietly. There was a desperate note in his voice, the slightest twist.

"What did you mean when you said, 'Right through the wrist'?" Rhan said.

Lee shrugged.

"I saw it, too," Rhan said. "In the parking lot."

The Iceman relaxed, just a bit. "Well, that's their oldest work. Dreams and visions. You have to remember, though, any images are pretty much symbolic." He grinned. "If you want real answers, you have to toss bones or gut a chicken."

If it was a joke, Rhan didn't get it.

"What happened to your dog?" he said.

Lee turned abruptly, but not before Rhan saw the change in his face. As if he'd been hit. The Iceman walked to the roof edge at the front of the house, then dropped into a crouch.

"He had her vocal chords cut. Because she barked too much."

"Your dad?" Rhan said.

"My dad lives in Toronto. And he's a human being."

Lee went over the edge with alarming swiftness. Rhan hurried to check, but the Iceman was moving across the office roof, heading down.

"I don't believe you," Rhan called after him. "I'm not just the entertainment. Whatever this is, it's got to be *for* something."

Lee didn't even look. He jumped easily to the ground and fished his bat out of the snow. As he walked out of reach of the yard light, he had the back and shoulders of a man who was leaving, but not retreating.

When Lee was gone, Rhan felt the relief run through him, and then a pang. The Iceman was strange, but he wasn't stupid. The bizarre theories had been...researched. It made him think there were books he wanted to read. And that he wouldn't mind having this argument again some time.

He began his descent. Without an audience he

was a lot slower, choosing footholds with care. He touched down cautiously on the office roof—the slant made him nervous—and peered over the side. Ten feet or so to the ground, but it looked farther. There weren't any more jumps left in him tonight.

He went down backwards, feet first, lowering himself over the ledge and dangling before he let go. He didn't fall when he hit the ground, but he sat down abruptly, facing the house.

The blow caught him on the right side of his head, an explosion of wet snow that was more shock than pain. Rhan wrenched around.

The Iceman was only five or six paces into the parking lot.

"Never turn your back," Lee called softly, "on a worthy opponent."

He loped away into the night.

THIRTEEN

RHAN dreamed of Chelsey. He dreamed that he found her wandering the streets, dragging her chain. Her gorgeous fur was matted and fringed with mud; her eyes were bright with hunger. She took one look at him and ran.

He chased her, wondering if he was crazy. He remembered how she'd come at him, a snapping fury defending her yard. She would have sunk her teeth into him and he knew it; a dog with no bark was all bite.

But now she was lost and running. And he was sort of familiar. If the Humane Society came for her she'd just be more scared.

He tracked her down to a dead-end street, backed up against a fence, her brown eyes trained on him in ferocious fear. When he was ten feet away, she began to growl.

"It's okay," Rhan told her softly. "You know me."

Chelsey's muzzle curled, showing teeth. Every step forward was a mile. Rhan realized it was too late to run; if he turned she'd attack from behind. He'd come too far, gotten too close.

"You know me," he whispered. *Please don't bite, Chelsey.*

And somehow he put out his hand. She sniffed it cautiously, hesitated, then bumped it with her head for a pat. Rhan dissolved to his knees in relief, running his hands over her golden coat that was suddenly silky again. She pushed against him and that was all the invitation he needed. He hugged her fiercely, his cheek against the warm, breathing reality of her.

"I know you," he said in wonder into her fur.

He woke up disappointed that he didn't have a dog, but the hug was still in him like an echo. And it was hopeful, somehow, the image of Chelsey restored. The past few weeks had been a battle in a lot of ways, but he felt that the worst was over. He could pick up his life.

Rhan lay in bed and ran his hands over his face. He was sixteen. Shouldn't this be any minute now? He'd known guys who were shaving two years ago. Maybe you had to practise first to encourage it. Except he didn't have any of the stuff—razor, gel—and he didn't know anyone who could show him exactly how you did it.

Missing pieces, Rhan thought. Locked up with that dead man nobody ever talks about.

The kitchen smelled like coffee, real coffee, bubbling in the ancient aluminum percolator Gran had brought from Vancouver. She'd finally weaned Zoe away from "that herbal crap." Gran was at the table, her curlers tied up in a transparent blue kerchief, mulling over ledgers. Rhan pulled a cigarette out of her package.

"Get out of there," she said, but not like she meant it. Rhan lit up and waited nervously.

"Raymond Siske," he said at last.

The name made Gran look up, suddenly alert. "What about him?"

"He had dark hair, right?"

Gran nodded.

"Well, did he have, like, a *lot*?"

"Why?"

Rhan grappled. "I mean, was he somebody who grew it...regularly?"

Gran looked at him as if he was raving mad. The jangle of the phone cut the kitchen suddenly. She got up and answered, still watching him until she realized the call was for her.

"Why, yes...yes, I did." She listened intently. "Really? Well, that's no problem at all. Ten o'clock? I'll be there."

She hung up and stood for a moment, her hand on the receiver.

"Jesus Murphy on a raft," Gran blurted. "I've got a job interview!"

The story tumbled out. A week before, she had applied at Bombardier, the subway car manufacturer, in the upholstery department.

"It's eight years if it's a day since I done upholstery—they must be desperate," Gran said excitedly. Her hands flew to her head. "Lord, this hair of mine! And my navy blouse, I don't know if it's clean!"

She almost bowled Zoe over on her way out the door. The shaving thing, Rhan thought, would have to wait.

◆

The interview had gone well, Gran told them at supper. She'd even gotten a tour of the upholstery department.

"God bless industrial equipment," she said. "It doesn't change from year to year. Oh, maybe the cutter's different—slices through eight hides like butter—but it's all still basic machinery. Nothing I can't handle," she finished proudly. She was hopeful they'd call her in.

"Well, it's not an emergency if they don't," Zoe said, stabbing at the casserole on her plate. "I'm not ready to put you out on the street."

Gran and Rhan looked at each other across the table.

When the phone rang at seven, Gran caught it before the second ring. But seconds later she held the receiver out to Rhan, an eyebrow arched. He took it, wondering. He couldn't remember giving his number to anyone.

"Yeah?"

"Hi," Kate said.

His stomach dropped and his heart went into overdrive. He motioned frantically at Gran to go away.

"Hello?" Kate tried again.

"Hi!" *Too intense! Calm down. You'll scare her away.*

"It's me," Kate said.

"What a coincidence. It's me, too. This must

133

be one of those parallel universe things. You know, I'm here but I'm there? You're here but you're there?" *Arghh...no! Stupid is worse. Stupid is terminal.*

"If you were here, I wouldn't have had to phone," Kate said, but there was a faint giggle in her voice. Encouraged, Rhan rushed on.

"Well, it's only a theory. And the phone company hates it. They put their money into the theory of relativity."

"Relativity?"

"You know, 'phone Mom tonight'?"

This time she groaned. "You set me up for that!"

"But you called me. It was subconscious. You wanted a bad joke."

"What I *wanted*," Kate said, "was to tell you it's payday. Your cheque is here."

The good news hit him like a bolt, and he was suddenly inspired. "Could I come and get it now?"

There was a second or two of silence. Rhan held his breath.

"Well, I guess so, if you really want..."

He made the six blocks in record time.

A guy he hadn't met yet was on the pumps; that meant Kate was working in the Snak Mart. When Rhan pushed his way in, the warm air fogged his glasses and he took them off. Kate was busy with a customer, and Rhan wandered nervously down the chip and cheese-puff aisle. Now that he was here, he didn't know what he was going to say. It was harder, Rhan thought, than when they didn't know each other.

The tinkle of the door bell made him look up. The customer was leaving, and Rhan noticed Kate watching him. But she hurriedly looked away, under the counter, searching for something.

It was an envelope.

"It's...it's only for the two days," Kate said as he approached the counter. "But our pay cycle is every Thursday."

He put on his glasses and tore open the envelope. The pay slip was in two sections joined by a perforated line. One side was the cheque and the other was a list of deductions, each with a cryptic code. His eyes darted from one side of the paper to the other in alarm.

"It starts off a lot better than it winds up," he said.

Kate laughed, and some of the tension seemed to dissolve. "It's a shock how much other people get, isn't it?" she said. "When I got my first cheque I nearly died. Here," she said and, leaning over the counter, she explained the deduction codes: income tax, Canada Pension Plan, unemployment insurance. The fresh and flowery smell of her almost made him dizzy.

"What about this?" he said, pointing to the letters S.I.N. followed by a row of X's.

"Well, as soon as you apply for it with Revenue

Canada, that's where your social insurance number will go," she said.

"That's a relief. I thought that's how many strikes I had against me in the sin department."

Kate laughed again and Rhan felt a leap of promise. He put the cheque back in the envelope but didn't move away from the counter.

"Thanks for letting me know it was here," he said.

A faint blush came to Kate's cheeks. "Dad would've given it to you Saturday, but by the time you finished your shift all the banks would be closed. The one we use at UniCity is open until 9:30 tonight. It's the shop account, so they won't give you any trouble about the cheque."

When he still didn't move, Kate got off her chair and began to restock a display tree of air fresheners at the other end of the counter. Rhan's hope sank. Take the hint, Van. He folded the envelope over and stuffed it in his back pocket, then started reluctantly toward the door.

"Are those new glasses?" Kate said suddenly.

Rhan stepped up to the air fresheners. "Yeah."

"They're nice." Kate studied the cellophane packages on the bottom prong as she spaced them carefully. "Did you ever see that guy again?"

"It's handled," he blurted. "Everything's... handled." Was he lying? He didn't know. But at that moment he was certain things weren't the same.

"My dad really likes you," Kate said shyly.

Rhan's heart kicked over. That's what she'd

said in the dream, his incredible dream. And the pine smell from the display was all around him. Like a forest.

"He's a great judge of character. He knows you'd have a great time if you went out with me again."

When she didn't answer he kept talking, desperately.

"It...it'll be completely different. A new and improved date. No money down, no money *ever*. Earn valuable Club Van points you can trade for luxurious trips and prizes—"

"When?" Kate cut him off but she was grinning.

"How about tomorrow?"

"I'm working again."

"What about Saturday, after work?"

Kate shook her head. "I can't. Patrice wants to go to this party and I promised I'd go with her. You know, moral support?"

Rhan didn't understand.

"Well, she likes this guy, J.R. ..."

"Payne?" Rhan said in disbelief.

"Yeah. Do you know him?"

Old friends, like old football injuries, could be conjured up instantly if necessary, Rhan realized. He'd go anywhere to spend time with Kate. She asked if she could meet him there.

"I'd drive you, but Patrice thinks it's going to be just us," Kate said apologetically. "Could ... could you pretend that you're surprised to see me?"

Rhan was bugged. Patrice again. But he wasn't going to do anything to jeopardize his second chance.

"Aye, aye, Captain," he said.

Kate beamed. "See you," she said.

He was flying as soon as he was out the door. That the world could change in twenty-four hours was amazing. He had money, he was going to see Kate again, and the Iceman...well, it wasn't the same.

Rhan felt fast, fast like in the old cartoons where the guy turned and the road turned with him. Last night the Iceman had come for a fight, but he'd let it go, thrown down his weapon for a race.

And on top of the roof, the Iceman had become someone else. Rhan didn't buy the ancient gods theory, but just to talk to someone about the power was a relief. It was something. And hearing that visions were only symbolic didn't hurt, either.

He was coming up on the mall—a warm and welcome light. He'd avoided UniCity for a long time but now he felt ready for it. The road had turned. And if road-turning was a skill, he almost had it perfected.

FOURTEEN

HE went to the bank Kate had suggested and opened an account. She was right—they didn't hold funds on the cheque. Feeling benevolent, Rhan left some of his money *in* the account.

"Live it up," he told the teller.

He went to the drugstore on impulse, wandering down the aisles like an uncomfortable tourist. He didn't understand why he was suddenly uneasy.

Jesus, Van. It's just a store. You've been in them before.

But he couldn't help feeling that everyone was watching him as he compared labels and read instructions.

Extra Protection Formula! Contains more friction-reducing lubricants for maximum protection against nicks and cuts!

Great. Have tourniquet on hand to staunch blood flow.

DIRECTIONS: Wet face. Apply small amount to fingertips, lather on beard.

Yeah, right. Rub it in, guys.

CAUTION: Contents under pressure. Do not place in hot water or near radiators, stoves or other sources of heat. Do not puncture, incinerate or...

You'll blow yourself to bits, Rhan thought. He put the can back on the shelf. He wasn't up for this yet.

He went to the place where he didn't feel like a tourist. Just to see, he told himself, turning in at Captain John's. Just to check the ratings, in case anything had happened.

Rhan clung to the console of Gemini Planet, weak with disbelief. RanVan was gone—blasted right off the screen—and the Iceman had climbed to number four. Number *four*.

"You got blown out on Tuesday," Sponge said, suddenly at his elbow. "Pathetic." He bit into a big, square chocolate chip cookie from the food court, scattering crumbs onto the console. "Offer's still open," he said, his mouth full.

"Hey, you!" the arcade clerk barked. "No food. Get out!"

"In a minute," Sponge called over his shoulder. He turned back to Rhan. "Ten bucks and I'll get you there. You pay the shot, too."

"No, right now, you little animal." The clerk started around the counter.

"I can get to the twins for twelve bucks—fifteen, tops—plus my ten," Sponge said hurriedly. "You got twenty-two bucks?"

The clerk grabbed Sponge by the shoulder. Rhan snatched the cookie out of the kid's hand and shoved the whole thing into his own mouth. For a brief instant Sponge looked stricken, then he grinned and showed his empty hands to the clerk. The clerk gave Rhan an evil look and let go of Sponge reluctantly. "Once more, guys, and you're both gone."

Sponge made a face at the clerk's back, then tried to edge Rhan away from the screen. "Okay, I want my ten up front," he said.

"Five," Rhan said, choking down the last of the cookie. "*I'm* doing this—you stand right there. Don't tell me anything unless I ask. You're...a consultant."

"Not for five bucks!"

"Take it or leave it."

Sponge hesitated. "You gotta buy me another cookie, too," he grumbled.

"I'll get change."

Hurrying back to Gemini Planet, his pockets heavy with quarters, Rhan felt a pulse of energy, urgent and excited, and strangely familiar. Where did he know it from?

That jackass isn't going to win. The realization swept over him. This was competition. The thing basketball couldn't wring out of him, someone else could ignite just by leaving his name on a screen.

Rhan positioned himself in front of the game, grinning faintly. He deposited his money and entered his code.

Never turn your back, Iceman. Here he comes.
RanVan.

"Hey, you're not bad," Sponge said, as RanVan cut his way deftly through the boulder maze.

"I know."

"Not humble, either."

141

"And you're not getting paid for opinions," Rhan said. He plunged his little knight into the quicksand and let him sink. "There's a door down here. What's on the other side of it?"

"The first ring...guarded by a giant. Six arms and sabres. You gotta—"

"I'll figure it out," Rhan cut him off. And he did, although it cost him a life to do it. But his second run at the giant he made no mistakes. Learn or die, he thought proudly, scooping the first ring of Ashtar out of its niche in the wall.

The second ring was in the ocean; the third on an icy mountain. RanVan was running on a sixth sense, anticipating patterns, learning and dying and learning more at a rate he'd never imagined. And yet he felt calm, relaxed. Like when you're still awake enough to know you're falling asleep, he thought.

"Holy cow," Sponge said, shaking his head.

The fourth ring was protected by someone new, yet Rhan recognized him instantly. A colossus of a man armed with sword and shield, arrows and bow. There was a regal aura around him; he had to be one of the twins.

"The good one, right?" Rhan said. "I can't kill him."

"Right," Sponge said. "Try and stun him in hand-to-hand. He pulls an arrow and you're dead."

Just then, the lights flickered. Captain John's was closing.

"Damn! Can I finish it?"

"No." Sponge was adamant. "Last level's the longest. But get this one. It's worth a lot of points."

RanVan lunged and darted for his life, fighting the urge to blast the twin with his laser. But he already knew this was one of the tricks to Gemini Planet: primitive weapons worked better in some levels.

"Descent," Sponge whispered tersely. "He gets ugly now."

"Guys! Come on!" the clerk called. RanVan leapt over the twin and snatched the fourth ring of Ashtar.

He just had time to see the standings come up before he and Sponge were hustled out the door.

"Pretty good, hey?" Sponge said excitedly, as Rhan paid for a square cookie in the mall. "Tied for number four. Never seen it, though—an identical score. I mean, is that a gazillion-to-one or what?"

Rhan felt dazed, as if he was still in the game or it was in him. He'd matched the Iceman's score—exactly. Yet he was still under him on the screen because the listings were alphabetical. At that moment he would have sold his soul for a single point.

"I want my money, too," Sponge said. Rhan pulled out what was left of his pay cheque. He had enough for Sponge and to pay J.R.'s cover charge and not a cent more. His next run at

Gemini Planet would have to wait until he got paid.

He peeled off a five and held onto it. "Tell me about the last battle."

"Well, it's your guy against the Twins in a cave," Sponge said.

"How do I know which one to kill?"

The kid looked uneasy. "You said you wanted to do it alone..."

"Which one?"

Sponge shrugged.

"You never beat it, you liar!"

"Hey, I could have," Sponge said defensively. "I was in the cave and both of them were firing on me, one on each side..."

"You have to let one kill the other," Rhan blurted.

The kid looked at him. "How do you know that?"

Rhan was suddenly certain. He could see it: the knight between the twins, the deadly bursts of laser fire flying back and forth, bouncing off the walls of the cave. The good twin would kill the evil one, if you could hang on long enough. You only had to stay out of the way.

Rhan thrust the money at Sponge and thunked him happily on the shoulder.

"Don't steal any jackets," he said.

"Hey, how do you know? About the twins?" Sponge called after him, but Rhan was unstoppable.

He went into the cold air lightly, listening to the snow squeak under his feet, drinking in a sky that was black and brilliant at the same time. The knight might be broke and a little behind in the shaving department, but he was on the road to glory. He had the planet figured out.

When Rhan opened the door to home, the voices seemed to strike him in the face, all the way across the house.

"You obstinate, straight-backed, close-minded...old lady!" Zoe said.

"Ha! The pot calls the kettle black," Gran retorted.

"You'd cut off your nose to spite your face, Lucille Petrasuk."

"On your face it'd be a blessing!"

Rhan was dumbstruck. He'd never heard his grandmother called by her maiden name, never heard adults fighting like this. Like kids, he thought. He hung up his coat and crept toward the kitchen.

From the doorway he saw the table dusted with flour and strewn with mixing bowls. Gran was wearing an apron as she leaned against the counter, her arms crossed over her chest. Rhan was alarmed. His grandmother only baked when she was mad. A fight with the phone company might drive her to cookies, or pineapple squares. From the smell of things, they were in for a pie.

Zoe saw him in the doorway.

"Here's an impartial judge. You tell her she's being a stubborn ass."

"More than usual?" Rhan said.

"Thanks a lot," Gran said.

"You can't give this woman anything," Zoe complained.

Gran flew off from the counter. "That's the word—give. Like the queen of England, handin' out favours to the *help*. Well, I don't need your charity, thank you very much." She looked triumphantly at Rhan. "I got a job."

"Great!" Rhan said.

"And I'm offering her a future," Zoe said. "A partnership in the Trail's End."

"Half of nothing is still nothing," Gran muttered.

"That's not fair," Zoe started. "We've got five confirmed bookings for next week, and two for the week after..."

"Like clean sheets wouldn't make a difference," Gran said with satisfaction.

"Oh, spare me the fifties bride routine."

"In my house you coulda ate off the floor."

"Because that louse Jack Van wouldn't buy you a table!"

Rhan's head was spinning. This wasn't an argument, it was a garage sale—old grievances tucked away for decades suddenly brought out onto the lawn.

Gran pulled on the oven mitts and turned stiffly to the oven.

"I...I'm sorry. That was stupid," Zoe said.

The pie thunked heavily on the stovetop.

"Don't let the past ruin the future, Lucy," Zoe said. "You're good at this and you know it." She hesitated. "If you want me to say it, all right, I will. I need you."

Gran still had her back to them. "And I need what they're gonna give me, Zoe girl. A health plan, and no-exam life insurance." She turned. "It's lymphomas. Or Hodgkin's disease. God damn it anyway."

Gran tossed the mitts onto the counter. One fell to the floor, but she was already gone.

◆

Gran was sitting in the dark in her room by the window, smoking a cigarette. She'd left the door open and Rhan didn't knock. There was a chair he could have sat on, but he didn't.

"What is this shit?" he said.

"Language, mister. You talk like a truck driver."

"Lymphomas, Hodgkin's—what the hell is this?"

"Well, they're tumours on the lymph glands ..." Gran started.

"Cancer?" Rhan demanded.

Gran nodded. She looked at her cigarette. "Should be lung cancer, shouldn't it? There's no justice in the world."

Justice. Like a steel-toed boot in his rib cage. He ignored it.

"So what are they going to do about it?"

"Depends," Gran said. "I gotta have a test gland removed so they can figure out which kind of tumour it is."

"What's the difference?" Rhan said. He knew he was being gruff but he couldn't help it. The words were just coming out.

"Hodgkin's has got a better cure rate. But they're both malignant. It just depends."

"Depends on what? What the hell does it depend on!"

Gran looked up at him, concerned. "Maybe you oughta sit down a minute..."

"I don't want to sit down. I want—"

Rhan stopped. He'd almost said, *To go home.* But that was impossible. Their suite in Vancouver had been bulldozed, scraped off the planet. They were trapped in this frozen, stinking bush town with a witch.

The answer was so clear it almost cut him. He shut the door.

"We've got to get you out of here," Rhan said.

"What? Why?"

"She's doing this to you, making you sick."

Gran sighed. "Little boy, I been avoiding this lump in my armpit for three months."

"Then she's aggravating it."

"Where do you think we're going to go?" Gran said, exasperated. "I don't know how long I'll be able to work—"

"I'll quit school," Rhan blurted.

Gran straightened. "Like hell you will!"

"You're not going to run my life forever!"

And then he heard himself. That steel-toed boot caught him again, between the eyes. Rhan turned and went out.

FIFTEEN

MOUNT McKay was a curse in his life, Rhan thought, as he trudged the long road to J.R.'s house. He'd always hated the look of the half-finished lump of mud, but now he discovered that the homes in its foothills were far apart—big lots filled with trees and brush that made great swells of darkness. And all uphill. Rhan could see J.R.'s place glowing ahead and above like a distant lantern. He felt like he'd never make it. If it weren't for Kate he wouldn't even try.

She was the only reason he was going tonight, all he'd let himself think about for two days. If he thought about anything else, the silent worry began to chew its way through him. Somehow he knew it would be better when he got to Kate.

Just to be in someone else's life for awhile. Or even next to it. Rhan wanted to hear long, rambling stories about carburetors and credit cards. He needed a dose of normal in the worst way.

"Glad you're here, bud." J.R. took Rhan's money with a grin. "Beer's in the kitchen, bedrooms are off-limits, don't punch any buttons. One of our friendly bouncers tonight is Terry." J.R. thunked a passing mountain on the shoulder. "But you can call him Mr. Make-Me."

Mr. Make-Me glanced at Rhan as if he were a stain on the carpet, then lumbered on.

"Nice guy. Human ancestors?" Rhan said.

J.R. laughed. "That's what I like about you, little bud. You don't care whether you live or die."

The expansive split-level house was already vibrating with people and music. Rhan had expected that J.R. would have a lot of his co-workers from the mill, but the flow in the hall was mostly kids from school. One girl from Laos's class gave him a bright but spacey smile as she squeezed past. There was some Chem 101 here, too.

He started down the hallway, heading for the kitchen. In the living room, he slowed to a stop, in awe.

The far wall overwhelmed the room. It wasn't an entertainment unit or a sound system, it was a floor-to-ceiling network of dials and speakers and screens. The largest one was on, twenty brilliant square feet, but the other shelves gleamed darkly, except for the neon pulse of digitized levels. The hand-held remotes were lined up neatly; a camcorder was poised on a stand.

The electronic jungle-gym struck a pang of envy in him, ten times worse than J.R.'s shiny black truck or anything else parked in the driveway. The urge to go play was very strong.

And not just for him. Rhan saw a guy reach for the camcorder, but he stumbled back with miraculous suddenness.

"This ain't no store," Mr. Make-Me said.

Rhan forced himself on to the kitchen. You're just here to see Kate, he reminded himself.

She hadn't arrived yet, though. Rhan took a beer out of a big cooler loaded with ice. He wondered how many he had to drink to get his money's worth.

He'd just wandered out into the living room again when there was a pounding on the door that drove right over the music.

"Police—open up!" a deep voice boomed.

An electric hush ran through the crowd; Rhan hurriedly stuck his beer behind him on an end table. He was under age—like everyone else. J.R. strode to the door looking pale. He made a wild motion at someone to turn down the music.

When he pulled open the door, the man on the other side seemed to fill the whole frame. But he wasn't in uniform, and he was grinning. J.R. sagged with relief.

"Reine, I almost pissed on the rug! Geez, you do a good cop."

There was a stir of uneasy laughter tinged with another sound; not everyone liked the joke. But as the man stepped into the living room, the grumbles died away. This guy was too big to be mad at, no matter how much you'd had to drink. J.R. made sure everyone knew Reine was the saint who had bootlegged for the party.

"Any of you ladies want to show your gratitude personally, there's a room down the hall," Reine said. "Line forms to the right."

That uncomfortable, taut laughter again. Backs turned and clusters formed once more, only now they seemed tighter. Rhan kept staring.

In his mind, he'd envisioned Reine Dahl as an older version of Lee, but there was little family resemblance. Reine's big-boned frame was well-padded; what didn't strain the shoulders of his leather jacket rested on top of his belt. He had thick dark hair and a moustache, and a stretch of five o'clock shadow you could sand boards on.

Rhan drank his beer without tasting it, watching Reine move through the crowded living room. When the big man picked up the video clicker and zapped through channels, Terry stood back politely. The Saint obviously had certain privileges.

And yet he didn't look natural, as if he belonged. He's just so...old, Rhan thought. Why would someone who was twenty-three want to be with kids who were in high school?

Across the room, Reine edged his way into a group of girls. Rhan couldn't hear what was being said, but a burst of high-pitched giggling broke over the music. Seconds later, Reine's big paw was resting on the unsteady shoulder of a girl, the one from Chem 101.

Rhan was squeezing the empty bottle. He could feel the Defender rising up, like someone getting out of a chair, and he fought it. She's not calling for help, Van. She looks just fine.

But he was coiled inside, like a spring. If it was Kate under Reine's heavy hand, things would be different.

"Well, well. K-Tel man rides again."

Rhan turned. Patrice had just come in, an explosion of hair and perfume and earrings that swept her shoulders.

"Where's Kate?" he demanded.

"Parking the car."

"You're so good to her," Rhan said.

"Look, she told me you'd be here. I've got something to say to you."

Rhan was surprised, and cautious. Patrice tugged him over to an empty corner, where he stood, self-conscious. He didn't want anyone to think she was his date.

"Katie's my best friend," Patrice started. "And I want you to know I'm looking out for her."

"So?" Rhan said.

"Maybe she doesn't go out with a lot of guys. Like maybe none."

She goes out with *me*, Rhan thought. "So?" he said again.

"Just because she's desperate doesn't mean she's an easy lay," Patrice said.

Rhan felt the disgust like a welt. "Lady, you must be real ugly inside, because so much of it oozes out."

Her hand whipped out so fast, caught him on the cheek with a stunning crack. Rhan staggered, knocked off balance by force and surprise. The room hushed, then burst into laughter.

All except Kate.

◆

154

"Why?" Kate's voice was a terse whisper. "Why does it always have to be like this? Why is everything a confrontation with you?"

Rhan had finally coaxed her away from Patrice and into the kitchen. People had stopped staring at him but it didn't help much. Kate looked like she was trying to fade into the side of the fridge.

"How come this is my fault?" Rhan said. "She hit me, remember?"

"But you do that to people. You...provoke them," Kate said.

"Some people need to be provoked," Rhan said.

"Well, why?" Kate demanded. "Why won't either of you tell me what this is even about?"

But he wouldn't. It was the only act of the night he considered the least bit noble.

Kate shook her head in frustration. "I hate this. I mean, all I wanted was to see you and have a good time. But I walk in the door and you're having a fight with my best friend...?"

"She's not your friend," Rhan cut in.

She looked at him, her brown eyes wet and angry.

"See? It's even with me. You jump on everything. No wonder you can't stay out of a fight."

"Everybody gets mad..." Rhan started.

"And they find another way to deal with it."

He knew that, dammit. It was at the top of his list.

Kate's voice softened. "Can't you just relax for awhile? Be...normal?"

155

The word caught him. He'd walked a long way tonight to be next to it.

"Let's go," Rhan said, touching her arm. "Just us. I don't care where but...we're lousy with other people. So let's just go, okay?"

He hated to plead. But this wasn't just any night. Kate seemed to sense it.

"Okay," she said. "But I need five minutes. I have to explain this to Patrice."

Five minutes stretched to ten, and then fifteen. Rhan waited at the kitchen table, impatiently smoking a cigarette. If Patrice was changing Kate's mind, he didn't know what he'd do. His ability to relax was wearing pretty thin.

Beyond the kitchen and down the little stairway, the back door opened. There was a draught of cold air.

"Shut the door!" someone shouted. Through the flux of people, Rhan caught a glimpse of short bleached hair coming up the staircase. The alarm travelled through him in slow motion, lightning turned to syrup.

Not today, Iceman. Don't be in my way today.

Lee didn't even take off his boots. Rhan stood up, his chair scraping. When Lee stopped alongside the table, he was close—too close. People were looking now, catching the strangeness as if it was a scent.

The Iceman looked down at Rhan's cigarette smouldering in the ashtray and grinned faintly. The cut on his face had almost healed.

"Smoke," he said. "Is that the best you can do?"

He scooped up Rhan's lighter and put the silver end into his mouth, thumb on the red lever. The room fell silent, curious. Lee pulled the lighter away and clicked it to flame inches from his chin. He blew a violent breath and a foot-long blast of fire shot at Rhan's face.

A girl shrieked and Rhan stumbled back. His chair tipped over with a bang but he caught himself with a hand on the wall. He was startled, not burned.

Thunder on the floorboards. The Iceman was just turning to look when Reine seized the front of his jacket. Lee's back hit the wall so hard, dishes in the cupboard rattled.

The Saint's eyes were dark and dangerous.

"Get the hell home," he said.

He thrust Lee toward the back door. Lee grabbed for the railing but stumbled down the five stairs, thudding hard against the wall beside the door. As he pulled himself up, his expression chilled Rhan. There was no surprise in it.

Lee yanked open the door and hesitated, looking at his brother.

"Son of a whore," he said. He bolted out— fast. But not fast enough.

Reine caught him in the back yard, in calf-deep snow. Half the house stampeded out after them but stopped on the patio. There was a single yard light that cast the snow blue as it was churned and broken.

Lee didn't cry out. He tried to protect his face.

Rhan was gripping the edge of a picnic table. This has nothing to do with you. It isn't your fight.

But it was no fight. Lee didn't try to hit back. He put his energy into shielding himself, moves so good they looked practised. Again and again Reine went for the right side of his brother's face, as if he was trying to reopen the wound.

The understanding spread through Rhan in a sudden sickness. This was not new. This had already been decided long ago. The gods were rewarding the bold and punishing the fearful.

Blood on the snow.

J.R. moved forward but Terry grabbed him by the arm.

"Let them settle it," he said.

The blue energy was roaring through Rhan like a hurricane, but he clung to the picnic table, holding himself still. If the knight took a single step toward this fight, he knew his vow would shatter under his foot like glass. And if he stood and let it happen, he was no knight.

Do something, RanVan. Do something *else*.

Inspiration. He turned and dashed into the house. On his way out again he nearly knocked over Patrice and Kate, who were finally drawn out by the commotion. Kate caught his eye—a frightened warning—but she would see. He'd found another way to deal with this.

As he charged into the snow, he realized that

he didn't know how to use this thing. But Reine wouldn't know that.

Just point it and shoot, RanVan.

Deeper and deeper. Reine had Lee up against the tall fence now. The massive back and shoulders nearly filled the viewfinder of the camcorder. Rhan pushed Record.

"Reine!" he called. Nothing. "Come on. Big smile, Reine!"

That did it. Through the lens frame Rhan saw the man turn, one hand still pinning his brother to the fence. Lee's pale face was smeared red— from his cheek, from his nose. Rhan gripped the camcorder to keep from throwing it. This is your weapon now, RanVan. Get it. Get it all.

"The camera!" J.R. cried. "My dad will shit!"

Magic was happening. Through the viewfinder, Rhan saw panic on Reine's rough face. He let his brother go. Shaken, Lee managed to grab the top of the fence and pull himself over.

Then Reine charged at Rhan. This wasn't supposed to happen. Rhan let the camera drop into the snow. He turned and struggled to break across the yard, but the wind-crusted drifts gnashed his legs. He felt a hand grab his shoulder.

You're dead—he's a lot bigger than you are, Van. But there were two terrible days and this night coiled up in his arm. Rhan swung around, fist up, and let them go.

J.R. crumpled into the snow, holding his face.

Rhan stared in dazed disbelief. From the corner of his eye, he saw Kate and Patrice running out of the yard.

SIXTEEN

THEY threw Rhan's jacket out after him. "You coulda broke his *nose*, you moron! You're lucky I don't call the cops."

Mr. Make-Me slammed the door. Rhan picked his jacket out of the snow. Dimly he realized he was still in one piece, that the smash had made Terry and even Reine suddenly cautious. As if they were dealing with a dangerous man. Rhan pulled on his jacket and headed slowly to the street.

The clouds had broken. Mount McKay was barely a sketch in the moonlight. Rhan stopped, unable to take his eyes off it. It didn't seem unfinished any more; it looked broken. Like a promise.

He'd tried so hard. He'd worked at being a knight and he'd *believed*—and it was for nothing. How was he supposed to help when he couldn't control anything? When he just wound up hurting people?

I needed a teacher, Rhan thought. And all I got was stuff in my way.

And what stuff it was. A madman with a base-ball bat and dreams exploding in his head. Never any answers about what it *meant*.

Yet he remembered how it could be: breaking the deadly circle around Sponge, overtaking the Camaro on the slippery road. The exhilarating rush that ran over fear and let him make the difference. Even tonight, when he'd turned the video camera on Reine. There was a weight to it, a power in it, like a sword in his hand. It had worked.

But not for good. He knew now he hadn't stopped that fight, only interrupted it. And the sickness eating through one old lady, he couldn't interrupt that, even for a second.

His guts wrenched. He gritted his teeth and held the liquor down. But other images kept rising up—Kate running from the yard; J.R. bent over in the snow. A single thought was circling in him faster and faster, the way you spun a marble in a bowl. There was no plan. The power was real and undeniable, but there was no greater strategy at work, no larger purpose.

It was as random as the video game of the gods.

"I won't do it." He said the words out loud. I'm not going to keep hurting people. I said I'd quit and I quit! It's over.

With effort, Rhan turned his back on the mountain at last.

The old Plymouth was just pulling to a stop in front of J.R.'s house. The engine cut and Kate got out. Rhan held his breath. When she started toward him, he was released, running to meet her half way.

Kate grabbed him in a bear hug.

Rhan was surprised but only for a second. He

162

wrapped his arms around her cushy softness, put his cold face into the warm collar of her coat.

"Where's Patrice?" he whispered finally.

"I let her out. On Flint, I think."

Rhan felt the revelation roll through him. It didn't sound like a friendly goodbye.

"We were going in different directions," Kate said. Then her voice dropped. "You know, I could understand her not caring what happened to you, but she didn't even care that I cared."

The hurt sounded fresh. Rhan hugged her and hugged her. He wasn't sure who was holding who.

"I know what you were trying to do, in the yard," Kate said against his ear. "I admire you— I really do. How come you're so brave?"

Hiding in her arms, he didn't feel brave at all. But he had to say something.

"Sometimes you just forget about yourself," Rhan said. "That's not really brave."

"But you're supposed to look out for yourself first. It's...instinct." She hesitated. "The things you get into really scare me. I can't live being afraid."

He heard the question in her voice, and the ultimatum. But he'd made a decision, too.

"Okay," Rhan whispered.

She pulled back to look at him, her brown eyes searching his face for a lie. He leaned in to kiss her and she met him so eagerly that her lips were a warm shock of joy. On and on he kissed her, afraid to let go. He wanted to stay here forever, wrapped in the safe, sweet darkness.

Light. His eyes were closed but he could feel it. Light like a tremor in the earth. No, I won't look, Rhan thought.

O, valiant warrior.

No—I don't want it.

We've long awaited your arrival.

Harder now, calling him, shaking him. The light was all around him. Rhan pulled from her mouth but he didn't let her go. He twisted into the beam.

The white Camaro had come from the other direction. It slowed to a stop across the street from J.R.'s house. The engine faded to an idle and the headlight stayed on—a single beacon. Rhan remembered that he'd broken the other side.

The driver's door opened. The light was reflecting in Rhan's glasses, playing havoc with his poor night vision. But when Lee stepped around the front of the car, he blocked the beam and Rhan saw the stocky, unmistakable silhouette of a compound bow.

The recognition made him flinch. Kate's fingers curled into his back, clutching his shirt. She saw it, too.

The Iceman was in full Descent. The blood looked like swipes of paint on his pale face, smeared by tears. What in God's name could make this man cry?

Lee glanced in their direction, then he looked at the house.

"Reine!" he yelled.

"Lee—don't."

Lee looked at Rhan again and this time he recognized him.

"You don't want to do this," Rhan said.

"She's gone," Lee blurted. "He killed her. He killed my goddamn dog."

Chelsey. The flicker of a golden dream. Rhan tried to take a step but Kate held him fast.

"No, she broke her chain. She's alive, she's just...lost."

"He said he'd put her down and he did. He's going to pay, the bastard!"

Lee tilted at the waist as he drew an arrow into the bow. Even from where he stood, Rhan could see the four serrated blades that came together in the point. It was a hunting arrow. It was not made to wound.

Lee took a few steps toward the house, then raised the bow and drew back his right arm, lining his eye to the sight. Rhan knew nothing about archers, but a cold chill told him this was perfect form. He tried to twist away from Kate.

"The police," she whispered. But they weren't here. They couldn't make it in time, by any miracle.

"Reine!" Lee screamed.

Rhan wrenched himself out of Kate's grip. The movement made Lee look.

"Don't get in my way, RanVan." It was a plea

but there was no mistaking what was behind it. The prince had been overpowered and was serving the forces of darkness.

Rhan's heart was trying to break out of his body. He knew how this would go. He'd seen it. Standing in the mall with Sponge, still drunk on the game, he'd seen what would happen, if he just stayed out of the way.

But he'd seen something else, too, and it was ringing through him. Maybe he'd been given an answer, a way to bend the situation.

"She broke her chain, Lee," Rhan said again, inching toward him. "She's okay, I saw her. Go look—she'll be there."

"Rhan, please," Kate begged. He was scaring her again. He was scaring himself. But this wasn't just a life, Rhan thought. It was two. If Lee killed Reine, he would destroy any future he had a chance at.

Maybe the Iceman was thinking that, too. His precision grip wavered. For the first time there was doubt in his wild face.

"It's my dog," he whispered.

"She's okay," Rhan said. "Put the bow down, Lee."

Lee lowered his arms, his grip still in position but loose, uncertain. Suddenly the door to the house flew open, a shot of sound on the quiet street. Lee flinched, startled, and raised his bow again. In that instant Rhan knew it was up to him.

The archer drew back swiftly, intent. And the

knight leapt toward him in a desperate bid to tackle him before he released.

Rhan was so surprised when he hit the ground. Wrenched around, as if an invisible force had grabbed his right arm, he spun and fell on his left side in the snowy road. He tried to get up and only made it to his elbow. He stared in disbelief at the four silver blades that dovetailed into his wrist, and the point that came through the other side.

There was no pain. For seconds there was no blood. His body, in its shock, forgot it was mortal. Rhan glanced up. Lee was horror-stricken, the bow still suspended, as if he were poised to shoot again. Rhan heard a shout behind him, from the house. They were coming.

"Go!" he called. It sounded like a croak. Lee hesitated, then bolted. Rhan heard the gutsy roar of the Camaro tearing away. Then there were people around, stricken faces jabbering at him. Rhan tried to listen but the edges of the night began to blur. And just before he passed out he finally saw it, all the blood on the snow.

SEVENTEEN

GRAN'S favourite comedian was Mel Brooks. She only had one tape, but growing up, Rhan had heard it a lot: Mel Brooks as the 2013-year-old man. He claimed to have lived before people believed in the Almighty, when his tribe worshipped a local man named Phil, who was so big "he could walk on you and you could die."

Then one day Phil was struck by lightning. And everyone looked up at the sky and said, "There's something bigger than Phil."

Staring at the lights above him in the operating room, his wrist a world away under regional anesthetic, Rhan almost laughed.

He did not laugh later. Gran pulled the curtain around the hospital bed as the doctor dragged over a chair for himself. Rhan sat on the edge of the bed, his feet hanging over, trying to ignore the strange weight of the cast on his wrist and how naked he felt in the flimsy hospital robe.

"All right," Dr. Arnason said, flipping open the diagrams. "This is what we had to deal with."

The arrow blade had severed three tendons and the median nerve of Rhan's right hand.

"It's what we call a mixed nerve," Dr. Arnason said. "It handles both muscle power and sensation of the thumb and first two fingers. It's pretty important."

Every nerve is important, Rhan thought, when it belongs to you.

The nerve and tendons had been re-attached through surgery, and he'd have the cast on to restrict movement for at least six weeks.

"Then we'll start on physiotherapy," Dr. Arnason said. "Sensation should come back in six months, at the latest."

"What about movement?" Rhan asked.

Dr. Arnason hesitated. "That's the iffy part. The nerve was completely severed. If the cells don't regenerate and muscle power doesn't return, you'll have trouble grasping and manipulating. Using a pen, for example. Also, the thumb has the tendency to drift up in line with the other fingers. Sometimes it's called simian hand."

Monkey hand. The mental picture gave Rhan his first thud of real fear.

"Are you right-handed, son?" Dr. Arnason asked. Rhan nodded.

"Well." The doctor took a breath. "We'll do the best we can."

Gran led him to the smoking lounge—two chairs and an ashtray by a window. She had discovered it when he was in surgery. Rhan moved clumsily to light up with the wrong hand and eventually Gran had to strike the match. He hated this already.

The window was dark and the corridors were dimmed. Rhan didn't know the time but he could feel how early it was.

"So," Gran said. "The big dog bit you on the ass and you didn't know until you went to change your pants."

"What?" Rhan said.

She sighed. "You got a talent, mister, for not seein' trouble when it's coming straight at you. How can I go when..."

"You're not going anywhere," Rhan cut her off. "Don't even talk like that."

"Talking or not talking," Gran said. "It doesn't make a difference."

She was right, dammit. This might be another one of those unbendable situations. Yet he couldn't stop the desperate urge to keep trying. He wanted to do something—anything.

"I looked at a suite yesterday," Gran said. "Not much, that's for sure, but you're in such a hurry to get out, you won't mind. It'll take a regular pay cheque, from both of us," she finished quietly. "But I hear that's what you want. And I know you won't miss Zoe."

The name seemed to kick Rhan from the inside. An idea was trying to beat its way out.

"I can't," he blurted. "I'm saving my money."

Gran looked at him.

"For college," he said.

For a long moment she was silent. He could see the disbelief wrestling with hope on her face.

"This is sudden," she said.

"Yeah, it is," Rhan said.

"What're you going to take?"

He didn't even think. "Something with cameras."

"We're gonna have to stay with Zoe," Gran warned. "We can't do it no other way."

Rhan nodded. She was the main reason for staying at the Trail's End.

"What inspiration booted your behind this time, I'd like to know," Gran said cautiously. She wanted to believe him, but she'd known him forever.

Rhan took a breath. "There's something bigger than Phil," he said.

Her lips parted in surprise and then she closed them. She put her hand over his left, the one that wasn't hurt.

"Nothing like a close call to set your priorities straight," Gran said. But the squeeze around his hand was a lot kinder than that. She looked at the window, at the first orange-pink crust of the sunrise. "I think I'll phone the old girl. Get her out of the closet," she said happily.

Rhan smoked another cigarette and watched the frozen mill-town skyline, black against pink. Maybe it was the leftover anesthetic, but he felt dizzy with a kind of wonder.

Something had happened last night. Pieces of his life had dovetailed together in a way that was just short of a miracle. And the parking-lot vision that had scared him so badly now struck him as a kindness: he'd been given the knowledge to make an informed decision.

And it had been a decision. Throwing himself at Lee had been an act of free will. Rhan felt a tremendous sense of relief. In dreams or otherwise, the knight would always have a choice.

In his mind's eye, Rhan held his list and crossed off the top line. *1. Perfect existing skills.* It had always meant control to him and he knew he still had things to work on—like his temper. But controlling the power—and deciding when it was needed—was somebody else's department. Somebody bigger than Phil.

◆

He'd never been to Zoe's room. But that night he went, his wrist throbbing at every step up the stairway. Whatever they'd given him in the hospital had worn off now, and the reality was rubbing him raw. He didn't know how he was going to sleep.

Zoe let him in without a word. He couldn't tell if she was surprised to see him or not. The room was filled with plants, astonishingly green and leafy, and shelves of books. Rhan felt a twinge again, that he was so...unread. He remembered that there were things he wanted to research, too.

Zoe looked at him expectantly.

"What you were talking about before, you know, about the commune..." Rhan took a breath. "I want you to help Gran."

"I'm not a faith healer, if that's what you're thinking," Zoe said quickly. "We worked with traditional herbal medicines and directing the body's own electrical energy...like air traffic control. It's no substitute for medical treatment."

"Well, you could try," Rhan insisted.

"She's going to resist," Zoe said. "She's a lot more accepting than she used to be, but anything...*extraordinary* makes her really nervous. It'd be a lot better," she continued, "if we all worked at this together."

She meant him, too. "Get real!" Rhan said. "I don't know anything about...I can't..."

"Kids today." Zoe shook her head. "You're so inhibited. You set limitations for yourself instead of stretching. Besides, you could use a little help yourself."

Rhan felt an uncomfortable knot under his ribs. He'd been thinking about what Dr. Arnason called the iffy part—monkey hand. Physiotherapy was at least six weeks away. He didn't think anything this old lady could do would hurt him in the meantime.

He shrugged casually. "Okay."

"First, you have to learn how to breathe."

"Yeah, right," Rhan said.

Zoe shot him a sharp look that killed the laugh in his throat. She stepped up close and placed her hand flat on his chest. He would have backed away but he was already up against the door.

"This is where most people think they breathe. But here," she laid her hand under his ribs. "This is your diaphragm. Now I want you to

173

inhale slowly, concentrating on this area, expand-
ing it as much as you can."

He felt so stupid. She must have known.
"Concentrate," Zoe said firmly.

Rhan closed his eyes and concentrated. It was
more difficult than he expected. There were so
many distractions—his aching wrist, the furnace,
cars in the street outside.

And yet slowly it began to steal on him, just a
relaxed calm that was nice, in a way. His wrist still
hurt but he began to think he might be able to
sleep after all.

When he finally opened his eyes, Zoe was smiling.

"It's a big world out there," she said, and then
she tapped his forehead. "But it's a bigger world
in there. Work on it."

Rhan opened the door to leave. "I don't do
closets," he warned her.

"No closets," Zoe promised.

He went to his room. The physical calm was
still in him like a pleasant tingle. All that oxygen
must have gotten the blood moving around.

He took his list out of the drawer. The second
line seemed to jump out at him. *2. Determine
parameters.* He'd written it meaning to figure out
where the edges of his powers were. But even the
idea of a boundary now seemed...limiting.

Better leave the possibilities open, Rhan
thought. And he awkwardly crossed it off.

EIGHTEEN

KATE had been wrong—he wasn't brave. Hiding along the wall of the strip mall across from Gervais Automotive, waiting for a car to pull up to the pumps so he could creep past her and into the garage, Rhan knew how much of a coward he really was.

When she was bending into the front end of a truck, checking the oil, he hurried behind her.

Mrs. Gervais was in the Snak Mart, behind the till. When she saw him, she glanced nervously out the front window at Kate. Then she put her arm protectively around Andy's shoulder. The warning caught Rhan like a wet rag. This woman had called him "love," but it was very clear who she loved first. Rhan had to force himself to continue on into the garage.

Only Moe was in the bay. There was a silver Pontiac Acadian with its hood open and a little rust on the passenger side. Rhan drifted over cautiously.

"I love these cars," Moe said. "No fuel injection, no high-tech gauges. Just simple machinery. I could rebuild this thing with a clothespin."

He slammed the hood. "How about you?" he said, gesturing at Rhan's arm.

"More than a clothespin," Rhan said.

Moe lit a cigarette. "They catch that guy yet?"

"I don't know."

"Pretty serious, not like a bar fight. You got a talent," Moe said, "for getting in the way of the wrong people."

Rhan couldn't stand it. "Do I still have a job?" he blurted.

Moe hesitated. "Well, the missus says no. I tried to explain to her I don't have legal grounds to let you go. Just cause, they call it. But she won't have you, and that's that."

"Okay," Rhan said, but his throat was closing up. He hadn't realized how hard he'd been hoping to keep this job, to keep these people. He tried to back away before the crash showed on his face, but Moe stopped him with a hand on his shoulder.

"You know, a friend of mine, he's got a store— TVs, stereos, all that electronic rot. He might need somebody in the back, or out front. You're good with the buttons," Moe said. "Maybe after Christmas we'll go see him, you and me."

For a moment Rhan just stared. This man was so good to him, he didn't even know why. Moe seemed to guess what he was thinking.

"You've got a good smile. Be nice if you could keep it." He scratched the back of his head. "And don't buy a car in this town until I check it over first."

Rhan felt the heat come to his cheeks. "I...don't drive. Yet."

Moe dropped his cigarette on the concrete floor and stepped on it. "Well, that much I can fix. When do you get that cast off?"

"Soon," Rhan said. As soon as humanly possible, or sooner. He walked out of the garage, light with wonder. Driving wasn't shaving, but it was in the ballpark.

There were no cars at the pumps. Kate was alone in the booth. Rhan was still nervous but suddenly hopeful. Maybe Kate took after her dad. Maybe miracles were in the air.

He tapped on the glass. She seemed to hesitate, deciding whether she'd come out or let him in, but finally she opened the door. The heater was going full blast and the small room was alive with the scent of her. It was like walking into a forest on a warm day.

"How are you?" Kate said.

"Healing," Rhan said.

She leaned closer, peering at his cast. "It looks pretty serious."

That was all the encouragement he needed. Rhan launched into a detailed description of the wound and the surgery, gory bits and all. A little corner of him thought it was a pretty pathetic bid for pity, but the rest of him—the part that cared about her, that wanted to hug her forever—didn't give a damn.

"And here," Rhan said, twisting to show her the underside of the cast, "this is going to be the real problem. Along here is the median nerve, okay...?"

She was watching his face, not his arm.

"It was the most horrible moment of my life,"

Kate said suddenly. "When you went down, I thought..."

But he knew what she'd thought. The memory of it was on her face like a shadow.

"Was it worth it?" Kate said. "Would you do it again?"

"Yes," Rhan said.

Kate shrugged and smiled—barely.

"I was really mad at you for awhile. That you didn't care about your own safety, that you didn't care how *I* felt...but it wasn't about that at all, was it? I mean, you weren't doing it to hurt me."

"Never," Rhan said.

Kate stared out the booth window, as if she was watching something far away. "You know, it's going to sound funny but...shy people never forget about themselves. They're always worrying about what everybody thinks of them, what everybody's saying. It makes you wonder what you could get done if you thought about something else for a change."

Kate looked back at him. "You're going to have a complicated life," she said. "But don't ever stop provoking people."

She wasn't going to be part of that life. Rhan felt the blow in his diaphragm, that place where Zoe said he was supposed to breathe. He didn't know if he was breathing any more.

Kate kissed his cheek and Rhan went home. In the quiet shelter of his room he blacked out the third item on his list. He didn't need any more lessons in pain.

◆

The police had never shown up at J.R.'s that night. They hadn't been called. Neither had an ambulance. Rhan had been taken to the hospital by Persons Unknown.

"Really good tourniquet, though," Dr. Arnason had said thoughtfully. "I've got to hand it to those St. John's Ambulance courses. Quick thinking, quick ride —somebody saved you a lot of blood."

The hospital had alerted the police, who had taken a statement from Rhan after surgery. He'd told them the truth—that it was an accident and he'd just gotten in the way.

They tried to convince him to press charges. Because the police hadn't arrived at the scene when the evidence was still in place, they couldn't lay charges themselves.

"If we could, believe me, we would," the officer said. "That was no toy. The Crown attorney would subpoena you to the trial as a hostile witness." His voice softened. "If you're afraid, son, we can get you protection. I think you know we're dealing with a dangerous man."

Rhan struggled. Part of him wanted to tell the officer about another dangerous man, the one cunning enough to hold his brother's car keys in one hand while he beat him with the other. But

Rhan wasn't going to bring up Reine's name. He'd already learned that the key point in the whole thing was intent. If he told about the brothers' fight, the charge of Wounding could become Attempted Murder.

"It was an accident," Rhan said again. "I just got in the way."

By the dawn of Tuesday morning, he was wondering if he'd done the right thing. He'd told the Iceman to go, but where did Lee have to go? What would be waiting for him if he went home? Or worse, what could be waiting for Reine?

He lowered the bow, Rhan told himself. He changed his mind. The shot had been a twitch of nerves, hadn't it? But he was haunted. Tuesday after school, he found the black truck in the parking lot and waited.

J.R. stopped when he saw him. Rhan felt the regret like whiplash. With the bruise-blue colour spreading out from his swollen nose, J.R. was hardly the cheerful guy who'd dogged him in the halls for weeks.

"Get away from my truck," J.R. said.

Rhan stepped away. "Where is he, J.R.?"

"How the hell should I know? He didn't go home." J.R. opened the driver's side with his key.

"Well, where *could* he go?" Rhan persisted.

J.R. thumped the truck cab with the heel of his hand and whirled around. "Will you screw off already?! Look, my family's kind of in shock, okay? So just...screw off."

Rhan was realizing. "You didn't know...about Reine?"

"No, I didn't! What do you think I am? I..." J.R. faltered. "I thought he was great."

He yanked open the cab door and got inside. He fired up the engine and gunned it with a vengeance. Then he suddenly unrolled his window.

"I don't even know why you hate me. I never did anything to you."

"It was an accident," Rhan started.

"You never even said you were sorry."

"I'm sorry," Rhan said.

J.R. glanced beside him at the passenger side. "Made a mess of the seat, too," he muttered.

The words hit Rhan in the chest. He knew who had saved him a lot of blood. It was not the kind of thing you did for someone you only wanted to use.

"The big dog bit me on the ass and I didn't know until I went to change my pants."

"What?"

"I can be a real jerk sometimes," Rhan said.

It took seconds, but J.R. finally grinned. "You're welcome."

It was dusk when the black truck dropped him off at the mall. Rhan knew he was only playing a hunch. Yet when he walked into Captain John's and Lee wasn't there, he was disappointed. The premonition had been really strong.

The arcade was quiet. It was the dinner hour.

He had no money and only one good arm but he went to Gemini Planet anyway.

He watched the cycle over and over—the premise screen, then the scoreboard, then the previews. The repetition was familiar and calming; the catastrophes were like old friends now. The killer trees in the jungle level, the surprise swamp on the plains. But there was something to get from every stage, Rhan thought, a skill or a clue. And you didn't move on until you had it.

Ice level. Rhan remembered struggling up—and sliding back down—the snow-covered mountain many times. Every inch of the thing was treacherous: the glaciers, the chasms, the avalanches, the huskies...

He blinked. There were no animals in Level Three—he knew that. And yet he'd just seen the vivid shape of a husky's head. The hunch was back, harder and more insistent. *Go look. Go look now.*

Rhan went. The wind gusting off Lake Superior made his eyes sting and froze the swollen fingers of his right hand; he hadn't been able to get a glove over the cast. He wished it wasn't so far, but he'd only seen one husky in Thunder Bay.

And what if he isn't there? Rhan wondered. What if you're just wrong again? Then you'll be cold and late for nothing, Van.

As he walked up to the Husky House Self-Serve and Restaurant, the doubt fell away. The white Camaro was sitting at the pumps, dazzling under the station lights. The golden Lab leapt from the front seat to the back to glare at him, but Rhan stayed back, out of her territory.

Lee came out of the restaurant, counting his money. When he saw Rhan he hesitated, uncertain.

"So now what?" Rhan said.

The Iceman seemed to relax. He walked around to the driver's side, cautiously. "After the sack of Troy, Poseiden kept Odysseus from getting home for ten years," he said. "Seven on an island."

Rhan was starting to know the Iceman's cryptic codes. "Where's home?"

"Toronto." Lee looked away. "I phoned my dad."

"He'll take you? Why didn't you go before, for Pete's sake?!"

Lee almost smiled, a grimace on his battered face. "Well, you know, the gods are always setting up tests. And you don't screw with destiny."

"But you're screwing with it now," Rhan said.

A brown sedan pulled up behind the Camaro and waited, its engine idling. There wasn't enough room to swing around to the gas pump ahead.

"You had the choice, didn't you?" Lee's voice was so quiet Rhan had to move in closer. "In front of Jim's."

Rhan felt his chest tighten. Lee Dahl had been provoked to change his destiny by Rhan's single act of free will. "You always have the choice," he said.

"But you knew what would happen, we both knew...!" Lee looked at him. "Then why?"

The Iceman was gone. This face pleading with him was utterly mortal and desperate to know. How could he explain why he had put himself in the arrow's path?

"Never turn your back on a worthy opponent," Rhan said.

For long seconds Lee just stared. Then the sedan's engine revved, angry and impatient. Lee took a step—Rhan thought he might turn on the driver—but he seized Rhan's left hand in a shake.

"You made me jump," Lee said. Rhan was surprised by the sudden grip and the words that felt like a prize. But there was something he had to say, again.

"We're not just bits of light," Rhan started. "It's got to be more than that..."

"I know."

The horn blared. Lee let go and pulled open his door. Chelsey danced anxiously on the passenger seat, but the Iceman looked back one more time.

"Find out what it's for, RanVan."

He swung behind the wheel and fired up the engine. The brown sedan pulled into the open space. Rhan drifted out to the road, watching the Camaro fade into the grey and white landscape. This man had made him work so hard, made him think and jump and stretch—and he was sorry to see him go. It was amazing what you could learn from the things in your way.

And how fast. The Iceman hadn't altered his life, but he'd accelerated it, Rhan thought. Moe didn't have to worry; he'd had all his bar fights in the past few weeks. From now on people were going to hit air.

Rhan turned for home. An idea was growing in him, becoming more solid with every step, until it had the size and weight of something real.

"Find out what it's for, RanVan," he whispered out loud. And the words wrote his quest all over the night.

EXIT 2ND LEVEL

To enjoy the whole RanVan trilogy, read

RanVan: The Defender

and

RanVan: Magic Nation

RanVan: The Defender

A flash seemed to catch in his left eye. When Rhan glanced out the plate-glass window, he saw that a silver car had pulled up to the stop sign outside the store. It struck him as odd. The sleek import was a long way from home in this neighborhood...

...in the next instant, the passenger door of the car shot open and someone tumbled out hands first onto the pavement. Black jacket, black pants, short black hair.

With a jolt Rhan realized it was a girl.

Rhan Van has never met anyone like Thalie Meng. She's seventeen years old, smart, brash, beautiful—and a mystery. Something is going on in the wealthy home where Thalie lives with her mother and Garry, her mother's boyfriend.

"Do you believe in evil?" Thalie asks Rhan. He does, and he knows he is just the guy to meet it head on. Like the noble knight in his favorite video game, Rhan pursues the Dark Lord in Thalie's life with a single-minded resolve. After all, she is a maiden in distress. Or is she simply trouble herself?

RanVan: Magic Nation

Get up! Stand up. RanVan.

Rhan pulled himself away, gasping, movement that made the room pitch. Who'd said that?

The skeleton was standing, looking at him out of black sockets.

"Get up!"

The blurred night pulled into sharp and sudden focus; blue lightning lifted Rhan out of his chair. The sky was falling and he was sober. He went right over the table, cups spinning, spraying beer. He charged onto the crowded dance floor, following the path that the skeleton made as he shoved people out of the way...

Rhan Van is in the adult world now. He's studying to become a television cameraman and hopes to finally find a place and a future for himself.

But the former video knight's powers have not diminished, and they soon lead him back to a confrontation with a challenging adversary. Before long, Rhan learns that the adult world is no game, because it is played with real lives.